In Search of
Dr. Dee

a novel

Jeremy Akerman

In Search of Dr. Dee
© 2023 Jeremy Akerman

Cover image by the author
Cover design: Rebekah Wetmore
Editor: Andrew Wetmore

ISBN: 978-1-990187-94-0
First edition July, 2023

2475 Perotte Road
Annapolis County, NS
B0S 1A0

moosehousepress.com
info@moosehousepress.com

We live and work in Mi'kma'ki, the ancestral and unceded territory of the Mi'kmaw people. This territory is covered by the "Treaties of Peace and Friendship" which Mi'kmaw and Wolastoqiyik (Maliseet) people first signed with the British Crown in 1725. The treaties did not deal with surrender of lands and resources but in fact recognized Mi'kmaq and Wolastoqiyik (Maliseet) title and established the rules for what was to be an ongoing relationship between nations. We are all Treaty people.

Also by Jeremy Akerman

and available from Moose House Publications

Memoir
Outsider

Politics
What Have You Done for Me Lately? - revised edition

Fiction
Black Around the Eyes – revised edition
The Affair at Lime Hill
The Premier's Daughter
Explosion (due in 2023)
Holy Grail, Sacred Gold (due in 2023)

To my darling wife, without whose tolerance and support this book
would not have been possible.

and

To my dear friend Robert Bockstael, who is always ready to assist
with suggestions and comments.

This is a work of fiction. While many of the historical characters existed, and some others, like hoteliers Ray and Janet Thomas, are real people, the author has created most of the characters and all of the conversations, interactions, and events those characters engage in. Any resemblance of any character to any real person in the present, aside from those mentioned above, is coincidental.

In Search of Dr. Dee

1

It was the year of Our Lord 1582, just before dawn, when all sensible creatures were abed and when the downs were at their bleakest. In the cold, dim light, the undulating land appeared as a series of huge, ancient beings whose eternal repose might be frighteningly disturbed by a harsh cry or an untoward move. Far away, like a glistening ribbon betwixt earth and sky, lay the sea, now, as in ages past, relentlessly hurling itself against the sands and cliffs.

There was no moon that night and dark clouds ominously tumbled overheard, unable to decide whether they should disperse or drench the countryside with rain. The wind driving the clouds also drove and flattened the coarse grass, and bent double the small bushes and trees whose branches were tossing restlessly.

A few leagues inland, where the downs commence to level out and clumps of oaks and beech became more frequent, faint flickering lights indicated the presence of a large house, the only one in the locality whose inhabitants were still astir. On the crest of the downs, silhouetted against the gradually lightening, steel-grey horizon, stood a circle of large, weather-pocked sarsen stones erected, for no-one knew what purpose, by men from many thousands of years before.

The first pin-prick of sunlight peeped tentatively over the horizon and made a feeble stab across the surface of the sea. It limped over the land and its pale illumination attained the centre of the stone circle. There, it revealed, barely visible, the figure of a man, the gale buffeting his long, black cloak with its pointed hood, as he stood arms stretched to the heavens in secret supplication.

For no others save he would dare to be abroad on such a night, this man must have been Dr. John Dee—or Ddu, meaning "black", as he was known in his native Wales—scholar, mystic, and adviser to Her Gracious Majesty Queen Elizabeth, who had blessed the Throne and the country for almost a quarter of a century.

The house from which twinkling lights could be seen was the doctor's own abode, but it would be hours yet before his return could be expected.

2

In the yard of an old brick factory, the filming of *No More Running* was winding down. Apart from a few pick-ups to be done by the second unit, this would be the last day for the main cast and crew. The many tents and trailers, in which most had been spending ten hours a day for the past six weeks, would be loaded onto and hitched up to trucks and taken back to where they had come from, or on to another film shoot elsewhere.

Only a few more scenes needed to be shot, and the bittersweet atmosphere attendant on the final day was everywhere evident. Much of the equipment had already been boxed and stowed in vans. People frequently glanced at their watches and anxiously eyed the sky for signs of rain.

The Director, First Assistant Director and the camera crew were intently focused on an area in one corner of a brickyard, where an arched exit through the stout wall almost became a dark tunnel. Just inside the tunnel, a small boy was eagerly waiting for his cue.

Standing some thirty feet away was Sean Dorch, the star of the movie. He was a tall, trim, handsome man in his early fifties, but his preternaturally youthful face made him seem almost boyish. An incipient smile constantly hovered about the corners of his mouth, and when his brilliant, blue eyes were not twinkling with amusement, they shone with curiosity.

"Going for picture," called the First Assistant Director.

"Going for picture!" The Third A.D. echoed all the instructions, but more loudly.

"Lock it up please."

"Lock it up!"

"Here we go. Picture's up."

"Picture's up!"

"Rolling."

"Rolling!"

"Roll sound."

"Speed," shouted the boom operator.

"One thirty-six, take three," called the camera assistant.

"Mark it!"

The camera assistant snapped the clapboard shut.

"Frame!" called the camera operator.

There was a slight, but pregnant pause, before the Director said, "And....action!"

Sean Dorch dropped to one knee and held out his arms to the boy. "Daniel! Over here! Come to me!"

The little boy peered out from under the arch, saw Sean, ran to him and threw himself into an embrace.

"You're safe at last, Daniel," said Sean. "There'll be no more running now."

"Cut!"

"That's a cut!"

The Director glanced at his shot list. "We're in the wrong place."

"Next scene inside the house," said the First AD. "Folks, that's a picture wrap for our star. Let's hear it for Sean Dorch."

Everyone applauded loudly.

Sean smiled, waved, and walked back to the hair and makeup trailer. He relaxed into the big barbershop chair while Sandy, the lead makeup, smeared his face with cream and, using tissues, gently removed the result.

"Are you wrapped now, Sean?"

"Yes, I'm all wrapped, Sandy. They are cleaning up a few odds and ends and we'll all be out of here." He yawned and stretched his arms. "I'm going to get a triple Scotch inside me, grab a plane, and go to see my lady."

"Sounds good," said Sandy. "My man will have forgotten what I look like, it's been so long."

"Nobody could ever forget your lovely face, Sandy."

"Hah!"

Just then, there was a loud knock on the door. Sandy opened it to reveal a silver-haired, saturnine man in his 60s standing by the step.

"Mr. Dorch?"

"Yes. He's here," said Sandy.

"Please excuse the intrusion, Mr. Dorch. I'm Ed Luvenstein. Your agent told me how to find you. Can you spare me some time?"

"Wait until I'm out of makeup," Sean said, a little crossly. "If it's important we can go over to my trailer."

"Certainly. It is, actually, important."

"Large blue one just across the way. Why don't you wait for me there?"

"I will," Luvenstein said as he bowed and backed away into the muddy yard.

"I wonder what he wants," Sean grumbled to Sandy. "Do you know him?"

"No. I don't think he's one of our crowd, but I don't know all the suits. There must be twenty executive producers on this shoot."

When Sandy had finished her work, Sean gave her a hug and a kiss and walked across to his trailer. Luvenstein was sitting by the mirror, and stood up when Sean entered.

"Sit down. What's this all about?" Sean was none too civil. "I've just wrapped a six-week shoot and want to get out of here to New York as soon as I can."

"I shall try not to take too much of your time. Am I right that you do not have another engagement lined up for some time?"

"I'm not clear how that's any of your business."

"Please forgive me. I should say that I'm acting on behalf of Harland Sollows."

"The director? "

"The very same."

"I've never worked with him, but I've heard a lot about him. Mostly good."

"I am glad to hear that. Mr. Sollows, is, of course, also the main producer for the film."

"What film?"

"Mr. Sollows would like you to consider a project he plans to shoot later this year. Mostly in Europe."

"Why didn't you deal with my agent?"

"I did discuss it with him at some length."

"Oh, you talked to Benny?"

"Indeed. He seemed extremely pleased with the proposal, especially with the financial arrangement. It was he who suggested I come here and find you today because I made him aware of the fact that Mr. Sollows is expecting an early decision."

"What is this proposition?"

"A most interesting one. I'm sure you'll like it."

"Please, stop talking in riddles. What's the role?"

"The lead, naturally."

Luvenstein propped his briefcase on his knees, snapped it open, extracted a script and handed it to Sean.

"Obviously, I'm not going to read it now."

"No, of course not. Please take it with you and read it tonight if at all possible."

"Tonight? I don't know about that. At least give me a hint as to what it's all about."

Luvenstein put his briefcase on the floor, sat back and put his fingertips together. "It's a historical film set in Elizabethan times."

"Oh. I don't know if I want to be leaping around in doublet and hose, saying things like 'gadzooks'."

"It's hardly going to be like that, Mr. Dorch. It's about the life of a very extraordinary man, although one about whom not as many facts are known as we would wish."

"That doesn't sound very promising," said Sean, sneaking a look at his watch.

"I think you'll find that it is," said Luvenstein quickly, sensing Sean's impatience. "What we do know is that he was a mathematician, an astrologer, an astronomer, a cleric, a scholar and a spy of considerable cunning and resource. He was also suspected of being an alchemist and a practitioner of black magic, including necromancy."

"Necromancy?"

"I believe it is the art of raising the spirits of the dead in order to predict the future, or influence future events."

"Who was this guy?"

"He was a confidant of Queen Elizabeth. His name was Dee. Dr. John Dee."

III

The slightest of hints of weak sunlight have touched the tips of the standing stones, indicating that it is time for Dr. Dee to abandon his rituals for this day, and to wend his way homeward. The flickering illuminations emanating from his house are not so prominent now as they were before because the sky has gradually lightened, but he well knows the way, having undertaken the journey many times. Every inch of the track, every bush, every rock is known to him as they are to the birds of the air. Despite his fifty-five years on this earth, he still walks upright, and his step is firm and decisive as he sets off at a lively pace.

A fox, intending to trot in a straight line towards the dunes, stiffens, spies the robed man, then turns and, at speed, runs back in the direction from which it came. Just ahead of him, some sheep, hunched into the folds of the ground, hastily stumble to their feet and charge away down-hill. Every creature hereabouts is familiar with this man, and every creature knows to keep its distance from his advance.

As he strode onward, the wind flapping at his robe, streaks of very pale yellow crept into the sky.

~

A few miles aroint stood the good doctor's home, a large manor house built in the reign of King Henry the Seventh, fringed by yews and surrounded by an ill-kept garden, save for the section devoted to the growth of herbs, which was well attended. A swinging, creaking lantern above the front door cast weird, intermittent beams across the earthen forecourt. From a window, a glimmering candle leaked its light onto the shrubbery. From afar, a cockerel heralded the approaching dawn.

Suddenly, a great rumbling and clattering disturbed the peace, and a large coach pulled by four black horses, gleaming with sweat, thundered into the yard and dramatically halted by the front door. The horses snorted and twisted in their harnesses as two richly-attired men alighted.

The first in precedence, a ruddy, portly man of some sixty-two summers, was My Lord Burghley of the House of Cecil, who was the Lord High Treasurer for England and Her Majesty's chief counsel on foreign affairs.

The second, a younger man by twelve summers, was Sir Francis Walsingham, who served as Her Majesty's Principal Secretary. He was minatory in appearance and, whereas My Lord Burghley liked colour in his dress, Sir Francis sported only black and dark grey. It was he who was widely believed to be the Queen's spymaster, controlling a ring of secret informants across Europe, and who had strongly counselled the close imprisonment of the Catholic traitor, Mary of Scotland.

The mighty oak door was opened and the travellers were admitted. They were greeted by the doctor's cousin, Tomos Jones, who himself was visiting the establishment, a tall, weather-tanned man in his forties with a distinguished, lined visage. He instructed the maidservant to take the gentlemen's outer garments and place them over the back of a large Welsh settle, by a stone fireplace in which a log fire blazed.

My Lord Burghley arranged his abundant posterior on the settle and held out his hands to warm them before the flames.

"Is your master not here to welcome us, Steward?" Sir Francis asked.

"Forgive me, sir, for I am not the steward," answered Tomos in a strong voice in which his Welsh ancestry could be heard. "My name is Tomos Jones of Llanbister, and I am Doctor Dee's cousin. I too am a guest in this house. The steward is aroint on some family business."

"But where is the doctor himself?" Lord Burghley asked. "Word was sent before us to notify him of our coming."

"Indeed, My Lord, he looked for you some hours since. When you failed to arrive at the expected hour, he was obliged to attend to some errands in the district."

"Errands? At this time of night?"

"The doctor does not observe the clock as most men do. No doubt you were detained at Court."

"Upon the road, in fact."

"Ah yes. Travelling in these times is frequently unpredictable. If you will excuse me now, I think the doctor should arrive soon."

With a bow, Tomos backed away from them and disappeared through one of two panelled doors in the far wall.

"I would he'd not be long in coming," said Lord Burghley. "I am weary to my bones. Something to eat and quaff would not go amiss. It has been hours since we supped."

"I'll ask that fellow to get us some wine," said Sir Francis, striding across the hall, mistakenly going through the wrong door.

After some time, he reemerged. "God's death!"

"What is it?" Lord Burghley cried, turning in his seat.

"My Lord, come here and see what I have uncovered."

Just inside the doorway was a wrought-iron screw staircase leading down into a large room. Half way down, Lord Burghley and Sir Francis started with amazement and revulsion at the bizarre sight which assailed their eyes.

The walls were covered with mathematical, zodiacal and cabalistic charts, while the long work benches were cluttered with a myriad items, including Mercator's double globes; quadrants; sextants; a Frisious astronomer's staff; jars of dark, viscous liquids; earthenware pots of nightshade; dissected brains; glass phials and cylinders; a large disk of highly-polished coal; encrusted crucibles; small woodland animals in cages; large jars containing unspeakable, murky, foetus-like figures; weird cantilevered models; skeletons of various creatures; a stuffed wolf; a dried mandrake plant; rows of bottles stopped with cloth and, in pride of place on a special stand, a crystal ball of smoky, white quartz.

"Be these things lawful, Walsingham?"

"I know not, My Lord, nor do I seek to know. If the time should come, I shall have information enough for my purpose. I already have a source of intelligence in this household."

"You have him under surveillance? Great God, what manner of man are we to hold discourse with this day?"

"A man in whom our Sovereign Lady reposes great confidence, and whose services she will have."

"Why does the Queen rely so mightily on such a man? I recall that she even had him decide the date for her coronation, based upon his unnatural omens and predictions."

"I believe Her Majesty is in awe of his scholarship on many matters." Sir Francis said. "She is aware of his travels upon the continent and the dignity with which he has been received there. The ladies of the bedchamber tell me that the Queen keeps by her side a piece of a warming pan he is supposed to have transmuted into gold."

"Such things are beyond my understanding."

"The Queen is by no means alone in believing in suchlike. But come, we had best withdraw lest he find us here."

~

Visibility had increased as the reaching fingers of the day stretched across the sky, faintly illuminating the tops of hills, trees and rocks.

Within sight of the house, but at some distance from it, two shabby footpads were resting behind some boulders near the trackway. One scruffy fellow was asleep, while the other drank from a leather bottle and softly mumbled to himself.

Unsteadily, the drinker pulled himself to his feet, unencumbered and commenced to urinate upon the grass. He hastily redressed when he saw the robed figure of Dr. Dee approaching. He poked his partner awake and pointed along the track.

They picked up their cudgels and crept forward.

When Dr. Dee drew near, the footpads leapt out into his path, waving aloft their clubs and demanding money.

Their would-be victim halted, tilted back his head, removed the hood, and glared at the men. When they saw his face, they dropped their clubs in horror and, gibbering with fear, scrambled away down the slope.

Not affording them a parting glance, the doctor quickened his pace and strode towards his house.

4

When Sean was in the taxi heading for the airport, a feeling came over him which reminded him of his Irish mother's adage that "money burned a hole in his pocket." He remembered the sensation well; the jingle which never lasted beyond the nearest bakery or candy store, because it had to be spent.

What he felt now was a similar compulsion, in that he found, try as he might, he could not resist taking the film script from his bag and opening it. It might have been better for him, and all associated with him, had he never done so.

From the first page, he was riveted by the document, often reading a page over and over before proceeding. So engrossed was he that he was unaware the taxi had arrived at the airport, and the driver had to yell at him to rouse him from his study.

He paid the man, and wandered to the Departure lounge desks, reading as he went.

Later, when Sean's plane was airborne, and flight attendants cruised the aisles looking for regulatory discrepancies, they found most passengers asleep and some reclining, idly flipping through magazines. By contrast Sean was hunched over the script, totally absorbed by its contents.

One of the attendants stopped by his seat. "Excuse me, sir."

Sean did not reply, and gave no indication he had heard the woman.

"Sir!"

Without moving, and barely aware of her presence, he merely uttered a low grunt. "Hmmh?"

"Coffee, tea or something from the bar, sir?"

Without taking his eyes from the script, he almost imperceptibly shook his head and grunted again.

The attendant gave up and moved on down the aircraft.

When they had arrived in New York, and Sean had climbed into a Yellow cab, he continued to study the screenplay, frequently scribbling notes in the margins. As they came across the Williamsburg Bridge, the driver called out to him, "Nearly there!" But Sean ignored him and carried on reading.

The taxi dropped him off in front of his partner's apartment on the Lower East Side. When he was standing on the sidewalk, Sean realized that his erstwhile intense desire for Liz's company and body had dissipated. He now felt as if his coming home constituted an intrusion, an unwanted distraction from something unnamed, but infinitely important.

The apartment was fairly small, but immaculately and beautifully furnished with luxurious Indian carpets, an expensive sofa, extra-large chairs, and paintings on the walls.

Sean dropped his travel bag by the door, kicked off his shoes, took off his jacket and tie, and sprawled in a leather recliner while Liz poured him a large Scotch. On the floor beside his chair, was the screenplay, which he picked up and started to read every time Liz left the room to make preparations for supper.

Liz was a tall, good-looking, red-haired woman in early forties. She was extremely well dressed, both tastefully and expensively. She too worked in the film industry, but in development for a large studio. She and Sean met at an awards party and had been together, on and off, for some five years.

Liz's kitchen was separated from the living room by a wall through which a wide hatch had been cut, so Liz was able to observe Sean whenever she wished, without him noticing.

"Did you miss me, Sean?"

"I certainly did," he responded in a manner which was more business-like than romantic.

"Uhh-huh."

"What do you mean, 'uhh-huh'? You know I can't get along without you."

"In a manner of speaking, I guess, but I'm more of a convenience than anything else. A port in the storm."

Sean put down the script and carried his drink over to the hatch. "Liz, honey, that's not fair. I love you."

She looked at him for a second then leaned out and pecked him on the cheek. "Yes, in your own strange, self-absorbed way, I guess you do." She returned to chopping onions.

"Self-absorbed?" Sean muttered to himself as he picked up the script again.

"Did you wrap yesterday or today?"

"Hmm? Oh, today. I grabbed the first flight I could get."

"Was it a tough shoot?"

"What's that?" Sean did not take his eyes off the script.

"The shoot. Was it a rough one?"

Liz came into the room and stood staring at him. "Sean, are you having a conversation with me, or reading something?"

"Of course I'm having a conversation with you," said Sean, embarrassed, as he gently let the screenplay drop to the floor.

"What's that you're reading?"

"It's just something somebody wanted me to look at."

"A script?"

"Yes."

Without realizing it, Sean picked it up again and protectively held it on his lap.

"Give me that!" Liz snapped. "What the hell is this thing? Por-no-graphy?"

She wrestled it away from him and skimmed through the pages. Sean looked anxious, rather like a child deprived of its toy.

"Looks weird. What's it about?" Liz was frowning deeply.

"A magician. Liz, it's the best script I ever read. I've never seen anything this powerful."

"Do they want you for it?"

"Yes."

"To play the magician?"

"I couldn't play anyone else," Sean said strangely, "that wouldn't be right."

Surprised and puzzled by his tone, Liz looked at him and handed back the script.

Sean grabbed it and clutched it to his chest.

"You're going to do it. I know you're going to do it."

"I have to," said Sean as if he were talking to himself. "I have to do it."

~

Later that night, Sean and Liz were propped up in bed. On the floor on Sean's side was the open script.

"I don't know how long I can do this," Liz said.

"Do what?"

"Continue this…abnormal…relationship."

"What are you talking about? Abnormal? We don't do anything too kinky."

"You know what I mean. In the past, when I haven't seen you for months on end, when you did show up, all you wanted was to sleep, get drunk and screw."

"Not necessarily in that order," said Sean, trying to be funny.

"Whatever!" Liz said crossly. "Normal people do other things, too."

"We do other things. We go out to dinner. Or shopping."

"How often?"

"Er...I don't know."

"But this time it's worse. You're so obsessed with this...magician thing...you don't even want to screw or sleep."

"Look Liz, I've tried to explain this before. You have to understand that when I'm working, I'm going flat out—emotionally and physically—sometimes for twelve hours a day. It's an extraordinarily draining process. When I get a break I need to unwind."

"You call that unwinding," Liz said, pointing to the script which Sean had picked up off the floor. "Looks to me like you are upwinding!'

"Liz, give me some credit here, please. I'll tell you what, let's take a trip together."

"Where to?"

"Er...England."

"Really? Why England?"

"It's great there this time of year. You'll love it. Besides, are there some things I have to check out."

"What things?"

Sean said nothing.

"What things?"

"Er...I want to do some research on my character."

"I should have guessed," Liz said disgustedly, as she rolled over and switched out the lamp on her side of the bed. She pulled the covers over her head.

Sean lay there for a while, then quietly opened the screenplay.

V

My Lord Burghley sat huddled in front of the fire, massaging his legs and moaning about the tardiness of his host, while Sir Francis Walsingham paced impatiently about the vestibule.

Suddenly, the front door was flung open with a crash, and Dr. Dee entered.

Startled, Lord Burghley jumped up and Sir Francis whirled around.

Pushing the hood from his head and shaking the morning dew from his robe, Dr. Dee gave a bow. "My Lord Treasurer and My Lord Secretary, please forgive my dilatoriness, but when you failed to arrive as heralded, I set about pursuing some tasks in the locality."

"I marvel that you have had no sleep, Master Dee, yet seem so fresh," said Lord Burghley.

"It is the habit of a lifetime, My Lord. When I was at St. John's in Cambridge, I trained myself to work an eighteen-hour day, allowing four only for sleep and two for meals and leisure."

"Could all men do as you, our nation's accomplishment would be prodigious," said Sir Francis.

"I thank you for your kindness, Sir Francis. I apologize that my wife could not have come to bid you welcome, but she is confined, expecting our fourth child."

"Your cousin was civil in your place."

"I'm glad of it. But, sirs, you come from our Sovereign Lady?"

"We do sir, or we would not have travelled so far with so little comfort," Lord Burghley said. "It was but an hour's ride when you dwelt at Mortlake."

"Again, I ask your pardon. I have recently taken this place because my house at Mortlake was burned by the mob."

"We had heard of it," said Walsingham, a little embarrassed.

"All my possessions, including my Greek and Latin manuscripts, were destroyed! Why? Because ignorant fools put it about that I was a sorcerer!"

The doctor's eyes flashed as turned on Lord Burghley. "Do you believe such slander, My Lord? That I am a sorcerer?"

"By no means, Master Dee. Were that so, Her Majesty would surely not love you as she does. Nor would she entrust you with the conduct of her especial affairs."

"For my part, I am devoted to the Queen. She may command me for anything that is within my power. I know she loves me. That much is evident from the tasks with which she charges me from time to time. But I cannot help but wish she might show it more often in some tangible way."

As men on the street being accosted by a beggar know, Lord Burghley and Sir Francis, too, knew what was to come and shifted uneasily in their seats. They cast their eyes downwards.

"I suppose you know, My Lord Treasurer, that of the hundred pounds she promised me at Christ Mass, but fifty arrived?"

"I had heard it was so. Alas, I know not the reason."

"And now I am cut off from the revenues of my holdings in Worcestershire, the lands which were given to me by King Henry. And all because of some pettifogging administrative order issued when I was abroad." Dr. Dee was now greatly heated, and moved about the room like a man possessed.

Glancing at each other out of the corners of their eyes, his guests wondered how they might stem the flow of his claims of injustice and broach the matter on which they had come.

"Is this any way to repay one who is so loyal, so faithful to the Queen?"

No answer came.

"Have I slaved and studied at five universities to be treated like a poor relation begging for scraps at the table? Have I counselled Her Majesty in the great sciences, taught her the principles of mathematics, communicated to her marvellous secrets known to few men, in order to be used so ill?"

"Master Dee," said Lord Burghley quietly, "I am aware of your feelings on these matters. You have sent me many letters."

"Indeed, many letters! Letters which, even when they were answered, produced little fruit that could be eaten."

My Lord Burghley's patience was wearing thin and, from the appearance of his visage, it was evident that, were it not for the Queen's affection for him, he would have had this man seized and flung into prison.

"I swear this to you, My Lord, that in zeal of learning and knowledge, and in toil of body and mind over many years, I know most assuredly that this land never bred a man whose account can be proved greater than mine. Nor with any greater love for his monarch."

Lord Burghley's face darkened, but remembering that they were here to seek further services from Dr. Dee, he decided that diplomacy was the wiser course. "Upon my word, Master Dee, I shall communicate all this to the Queen and advise her to rectify this manifest injustice."

"Your kindness does you great credit, My Lord."

Suddenly, Dr. Dee had become almost a different person. He smiled and clapped his hands, whereupon a withered and bent maid-servant entered.

"Go with this woman, and she will conduct you to a chamber where you may wash and attend to your attire. In half an hour we shall gather in my study, where you can tell me the burden of your mission over a hearty breakfast."

~

The sun was up, and the cockerel had crowed many times when they gathered to break their fast. The doctor's study was a large, wood-panelled room, with a large window looking out onto the downs. There, crows were swooping and cawing, whilst sheep were slowly grazing.

Where they were not occupied by book-laden shelves, the walls bore astronomical tables and charts of chemical formulae. In one corner was an owl chained to its perch; in another, a raven similarly restrained. Both coldly blinked at the proceedings unfolding before them.

At a stout, oak table underneath the window, Lord Burghley, Sir Francis and Doctor Dee made short work of their repast of bread and slabs of fried meat, accompanied by tankards of ale.

"A plot to murder the Queen!" exclaimed the doctor, when his guests had outlined their mission. "The very highest kind of treason."

"If it is true," said Sir Francis. "We have just one piece of evidence to date. The letter which was lost, and found by my agents."

"But," said Burghley, "since Master Dee has deciphered the letter himself and we have independently arrived at a virtually identical content for the missive, I fear there can be no doubt."

"Who was your decryptor?"

"Thomas Fowles. He consulted your *Monas Hierogylphica* and followed the methods you set out in that book."

"So indeed there is no doubt. You do not know from whom the letter came, nor to whom it was sent. Nor yet who carried it."

"Alas, nor nothing else about it save that either the sender or the intended recipient has high position at Court."

"Or both of them do."

The raven uttered a loud croak.

"That did not occur to you?"

"We assumed that if both were at Court, they could have communicated through ordinary discourse," said Lord Burghley.

"It is likely, but we must rule out nothing. How and where may I best serve the Queen in this affair?"

"In your contacts abroad," said Sir Francis, "and with those who come from and go to far places. It is clear from the letter that some manner of foreign intervention is crucial to the success of the plot. As you are probably aware, my own ring of spies is formidable in France, Italy and the Low Countries; but I have not yet the same capacity in Spain, Saxony and Poland, where I believe you are well-connected."

Dr. Dee nodded his assent.

"Therefore, anything you might hear, however slight, should be brought to my attention immediately."

"Very well," declared Dr. Dee, rising. "It shall be done! Please inform the Queen that I shall not rest, nor shall my inquiries cease, until we have this vile traitor, root and branch."

6

When Sean woke in the morning, it was already late. Sun was streaming through the windows and the noise of traffic drifted up from the city streets.

He yawned, stretched, rubbed his eyes then rolled over on his side. Propped up on Liz's night table was a note, which he grabbed and opened.

> *Sean: This is not going to work. Will be staying with Peggy until you go. Maybe we will talk when you get back from England. Do not try to call me at work. Liz.*

Cursing, Sean crumpled the note and hurled it across the bedroom. He sat fuming on the edge of the bed, trying to decide what to do.

Of course, he would do the one thing she had specifically asked him not to. He snatched up his phone and dialed her office. "Diane, this is Sean. I don't care what she told you. You'd better put her on. Tell her if she won't speak to me, I'll come over there and create a scene. And I'm good at creating scenes. It's what I do for a living."

"Oh, God, Sean. Alright."

"Smart move, Diane."

Sean punched up the pillows and lay back on the bed.

"This is not a good idea," Liz said when she came on the line.

"What the hell is going on? Just walking out on me like that?"

"Go away, Sean. Go to England. Go to Mars, for all I care. I'll talk to you when you get back."

"Why are you doing this?"

"I don't think I really know you. Maybe I never did. I'm not so sure I want to. Goodbye. Sean."

Then she was gone.

Sean swore and pounded the counterpane with his phone. It jumped out of his hand and fell off the bed. When he leaned over to retrieve it, he saw the screenplay lying there.

Instantly, he was diverted and picked it up. He turned to the cover, where Ed Luvenstein's number was written, then punched in the number.

"Mr. Luvenstein, this is Sean Dorch."

"Ah yes, Mr. Dorch. How are you?"

"Yes, I'm okay, thanks. Listen, you can tell Mr. Sollows I'll do it. You can work out the details with Benny, my agent. You have his number."

"Yes, I do. This is very good news. Mr. Sollows will be pleased."

"There's just one condition."

"Oh yes?"

"I want the supporting role to go to a good friend of mine."

"Oh, I don't know about that—"

"He's a very good actor. I vouch for him. I'll email you his re-sume."

"I can look him up myself on IMDb," said Luvenstein. "What's his name?"

"Tom Johnson. He's currently working out of Nova Scotia."

"Mr. Sollows likes to pick his own cast, unless a studio imposes someone. That would only happen with a well-known star which, clearly, your friend is not, otherwise I would recognize his name."

"Tell Sollows that's my condition."

"I'll tell him, but speaking frankly, he's not the kind of man who likes to be dictated to. More than likely he'll to tell you to take your friend and fuck off."

"If he does, he does. This is a huge, demanding role, and I need the support of someone I know and have worked with before."

"You won't change your mind? I really think you should."

"No, I won't."

"Okay. I'll get back to you as soon as I get hold of him."

Once shaved and dressed, Sean sat at Liz's table having a cup of coffee and a sandwich. The script lay open at his right hand, and he re-read page after page mesmerically, until the ringing of the telephone startled him.

"This is your lucky day." It was Luvenstein.

"Oh yeah?"

"I have to say I didn't expect he would go for it, but it won't be a problem. He did some research and asked around about your friend and, apparently, he got a satisfactory response."

"Good. That's fantastic. Thanks for letting me know. I presume I will see you again in September when we do the shoot."

"I imagine you will, Mr Dorch."

~

Tom Johnson's apartment in Halifax was neither fancy nor commodious, but it had a spectacular view of the harbour from the balcony. Tom was leaning on the rail, gazing out to sea and enjoying the unusually-windless weather. He was a slightly younger man than Sean, not as tall, but more tanned and athletic.

Theirs had been a strange relationship, very friendly, but marked by a number of instances when Tom had felt it necessary either to restrain Sean, or extract him from some kind of trouble. When sober, Sean was wonderful company and was intelligent, funny and engaging. But Sean could also be a heavy drinker, and when he had too much, which was often, he could become paranoiac, belligerent and sometimes impossible to handle.

They had met on the set of a film some ten years previously, and maintained contact ever since. Now, they were almost like brothers and got together whenever they could.

Tom was not surprised to hear from Sean, but he certainly was amazed to learn about the movie. "This is hard to believe. Are you sure about this?"

"Absolutely," said Sean, "It's done and dusted. Don't tell me there's a conflict. You don't have anything in the pipe, do you?"

"No. Actually, I'm going through a dry period."

"Why don't I come there? We can catch up before we go to England."

"Whoa! England?"

"Yes, I thought it would be good if we could go over there and track down where these characters were. Get into their heads, that kind of thing."

"Is the production paying for this junket?"

"No, I am. I made a small fortune on *No More Running*."

"Well, I'd have to be subsidized to some extent. If you're sure."

"What are friends for? We'll have a blast."

"Alright, then. When shall I expect you?"

"Tomorrow. There's a flight from Newark Liberty arriving at 4:20."

"Wow. You don't hang about!"

"We have a lot of talking to do, so I don't want to book into a hotel. Can I have your couch for a few days?"

"I'll even get clean sheets for it."

VII

On the morrow, having breakfasted and imparted the nature of their mission, Lord Burghley and Sir Francis were anxious to return to London. In truth, it might be more accurate to say that they could not take their leave soon enough.

"That fellow gives me the shudders," observed Lord Burghley when they were upon the Horsham Road.

"Marry, he is a strange one, I declare," said Sir Francis. "I own that, were he not a favourite of Her Majesty, I should have him under close arrest for examination."

"I was informed that some years ago he was charged with treason."

"That is true, My Lord, but that was under the Catholic regime, so we cannot hold it against him now. That he was persecuted by her sister would only endear him to the Queen even more."

"Indeed. Methinks it is a good thing that Her Majesty has reigned for almost a quarter of a century. When monarchs change, much changes with them, and it is hard for a man to know which way to jump."

"Fortune favours us that Her Majesty has had a long reign, and is still in robust health."

"Walsingham, whom do you suspect of being our traitor?"

"There are five of whom I am suspicious, but I hasten to say that I have no proof of disloyalty on the part of any of them."

"Are you at liberty to share their names with me? If I am also to keep my eyes and ears open, I need to know where to look and listen."

"Your Lordship makes a sound point." Walsingham admitted. "But the names must be for you and you alone."

"I give you my word, they shall not go any further."

"Not even to the Queen."

"Well…er…"

"My Lord, if the Queen hears these names before we have any solid evidence against them, she might lose her temper and in a fit of pique, might order innocent men to their deaths."

"Ah. I had not thought of that. Very well, it shall be as you say. Between the two of us only."

"The five are the Earl of Leicester, always out to make trouble—"

"Indeed!"

"Sir John Scudamore. He is a shifty fellow at the best of times."

"An interesting prospect."

"Howard, Earl of Northampton. I swear the man has been a Catholic all his life and cleaves to that faith yet."

"But, sadly, we have never been able to prove it."

"Sir Edward Luvington."

"Why he, Walsingham?"

"He is too nice, too obliging, and too ready to declare his loyalty."

"And the fifth?"

"Our old friend Sir Walter Raleigh."

"Raleigh?!"

"He travels in foreign parts. He meets many strange people. He comes and goes at will. I cannot afford to trust someone like that."

"Of course, it may be none of the names on your list," said Lord

Burghley glumly.

"Alas, that is true. We will have to wait and see what my agents and Master Dee's contacts produce. We may find it is someone we would least suspect."

~

Dr. Dee and his cousin, Tomos, watched as the grandee's coach trundled out of the yard and along the distant highway.

"Do I take it that your guests were important men, cousin?" Tomos asked.

"The most important in the land, save for the Queen herself."

"You should be the more flattered that they should come so far, when they might have summoned you to London."

"My presence in London would give rise to unwelcome speculation. After the outrage at Mortlake, I doubt the Queen wants it widely known that she calls upon my services."

"You may not be able to tell me, and that I should remain ignorant, but the matter about which those men came here must be some great secret affair of state."

"You have guessed aright. Cousin Tomos, walk with me awhile and I will tell you everything."

They walked out of the property and out on to the downs. The sun shone strongly, making the day pleasant, and the great grassy downs spread out before them. The turf beneath their feet was firm and dry. In the distance, the sea sparkled, a tiny reflection springing from every wave.

They strolled along the ridgeway which tacked over the crest of the downs. A gentle breeze barely ruffled Dr. Dee's robe. At length, he described the mission of their Lordships and adumbrated the problem they faced.

"As earnest and eager as I am to catch and dispatch this villain who would assassinate the Queen, I have mixed feelings when it comes to matters of treason. Does that surprise you?"

"Marry, it does. But if it is so, cousin, I warrant there is some personal reason for it."

Suddenly, the doctor stopped and raising his arm pointed to the sky. "Tomos, look there!"

Tomos followed his cousin's directions and saw a hovering kestrel, suspended in position, scouring the ground for prey.

"Shall we see him dive, I wonder?"

"Maybe," said Dr. Dee, "but he can stay aloft, in the same place, for hours on end."

"He would make a good spy, methinks."

"You have read my mind, cousin."

After a while they came to a stream and, like small boys, sat astride a large tree trunk which had fallen across, and dangled their legs. The doctor trailed a long stick in the water, while Tomos threw pebbles into the current.

"You guessed aright when you said I had a personal reasons for being somewhat ambivalent about accusations of treason. I was once accused of treason myself."

"In Wales, we seldom hear about intrigues at court. But I recall that some years since there were some whispers to the effect that you had incurred the displeasure of Her Majesty."

"That was in Queen Mary's time. Because I was corresponding with Princess Elizabeth on scholarly matters, I was denounced as a traitor. My accusers said I had tried to take the Queen's life by poison and magic. One day at Hampton Court, I was seized, dragged to jail and left to rot. Can you imagine such injustice? Me, a Doctor of Divinity, treated like a common criminal! The cell was cold, damp and dark, the only light coming from a tiny opening high in the slimy stone wall.

"After many days of solitude, during which I was supposed to reflect upon my so-called crimes, I was told I was to be examined by the Secretary of State, Sir John Bourne. Although he questioned me for nearly two days, alas, Sir John was unsatisfied with my answers because I refused to admit guilt.

"So he had me dragged before the Privy Council. But I was more of a disappointment to those gentlemen than I had been to Sir John. Where they failed, they thought Lord Brooke would succeed. He was Chief Judge of Common Pleas. And when he, too, failed to get what answers they desired, they took me to the Star Chamber, a court from whose arbitrary and unaccountable decisions few men ever escaped with their liberty."

"But, obviously, you did escape or you would not be here to tell the tale," said Tomos.

"It was a long trial, but eventually I was discharged of all suspicion of treason."

"What a torment you must have endured."

"Stay! I am not finished." Dr. Dee hurried on with his narrative. "I was acquitted of treason, but not of heresy. Since none there could say what heresy was, they bound me over to the custody of the Bishop of London, and put me in his prison."

Dr. Dee pulled off his boots and slid off the tree into the brook. He splashed downstream, holding his robe about his waist.

"No doubt, cousin, you are beginning to think this story will never end."

"I had wondered. You certainly have more satisfaction in relating these experiences than you did in living them. But since you are free, alive and well, I conclude that you were again acquitted."

Laughing, Dr. Dee climbed onto the bank, wiped his feet on the grass and pulled on his boots. "Yes, but only after months of resisting their efforts to entrap me. They put me into the same cell as the heretic Barthlet Green—"

"The one who was burned at the stake?"

"The very same. They thought my sympathies for Green as a man would cause me also to voice support for his heresies."

"But his crime was for being a Protestant. Burned alive for that! Today we would all go to the stake!"

"Indeed. But they had not finished with me yet. They employed me in the examination of another heretic, one Philpot. They thought the way I framed my questions to him would reveal my own heretical views. Finally, I was released, but even then only by special decree of the Queen and Prince Philip of Spain."

"Alas, so many similar stories could be told of men who have pushed at the edges of scholarship, or challenged the convention wisdom of the age."

"That is surely true," Dr. Dee concurred.

"I trust that your own experiences will temper your zeal in this affair of the Queen's," Tomos said earnestly. "If you have a condemnatory report to give Walsingham. I hope you will make completely sure you have the right man. If you make a mistake, the tide could bring it back to your door."

Dr. Dee gave Tomos a sharp glance. The two men then retraced their steps across the downs. The wind was rising a little and clouds were started to move into the blue sky.

~

But a few miles from Dr. Dee's house was a small, rustic cottage hunched into a cleft in the sloping land. Around the dwelling were patches of vegetables and tethered animals. One was a tiny donkey, the other a nanny goat. A boy of not yet twenty summers was mending a rickety fence and, some yards away, his sister, Thomasina, was spreading washed clothes to dry on some bushes.

Thomasina was a verily comely, not to say beautiful, young maid of five and twenty summers, with a lithe, supple, almost boyish figure. She had full, mirthful lips, big sparkling eyes and long, gleaming, flame-coloured hair. This hair was not frizzled and carrot-hued, but was almost iridescent, as if comprised of alternate strands of scarlet and gold.

When she saw Dr. Dee and Tomos approaching, she hastily wiped her hands on her apron and straightened up.

Tomos was immediately struck by her beauty. He did not think he had beheld such a wondrous creature in his life.

"This, cousin Tomos, is Thomasina, who is about to enter my service."

"Indeed?"

"Yes. Hester is getting too old and infirm to discharge all her duties properly, and if Jane is safely delivered of the child she is expecting, there will be even more work to do."

"She is surely an entrancing wench. I hope her work is equal to her looks."

"I do not doubt it," said Dr. Dee. "Thomasina, I bid you good day. All are well here, I trust."

"Yes, thankee, Master Dee. All are fine, apart from my father's rheumatics."

"You may fetch more of that unguent for him any time you wish."

"Thankee kindly, sir."

"Thomasina, this is my cousin, Master Jones from Wales. I have told him you will be coming up to the manor as a maidservant."

"Yes, sir. I can start tomorrow if you wish it."

"I do. Talbot should have returned by then, so you should report to him."

At the mention of the name of Talbot, a look of anxiety mingled with disgust crossed Thomasina's face.

"Are you worried about the warning I gave you? If so, I shall not be offended if you choose to bide with your family."

"No 'tis not that, sir," said Thomasina. "You can rely on me, Master Dee. I shall do as 'ee says."

"And you are satisfied with the sum mentioned?"

"I am, sir. It is very generous."

"Good, then it is settled. We shall see you on the morrow. Good day to you, Thomasina."

"Goodbye Master Dee, and Master Jones."

"I take my leave of you, Miss Thomasina and look forward to seeing you in the days ahead."

Thomasina returned to her laundering and the two men sauntered off.

When the cottage was out of earshot, Tomos stayed his cousin. "Cousin, I have two questions?"

"Ask."

"The first is: Who is Talbot?"

"Ah, he is my steward. Of sorts. He helps me with my, er... work."

"I perceive that Thomasina is greatly afeared of him."

"Really?" Dr. Dee paused. "Maybe. In which case we must keep a close eye on them. Talbot can be a coarse fellow, and Thomasina has beauty enough to tempt any man."

"That much is surely true," said Tomos with a long sigh.

"And your second question?"

"What was the warning you gave her?"

"I warned her that coming to work and live under my roof might make her relations with the local populace more difficult. It might serve to confirm their prejudices and superstitions, if not inflame them."

"What prejudices? What superstitions?"

"Hereabouts, is it widely believed that any woman with red hair is likely to be a witch."

8

When Tom picked Sean up at the airport, he wondered if his friend had been drinking on the plane. Sean seemed unnaturally flushed and excited, and was speaking at a rapid pace.

After the initial greetings, Tom found that he could not get a word in edgeways, so he just let Sean ramble on. As he maundered, he clutched the script tightly as if he thought someone would try to take it away from him.

"It's incredible! It's about an incredible man. Just unbelievable! You're going to love him. I know you will."

"So you said. Will I like his side-kick, too?"

"What? His cousin? Oh, yes, of course. He's a good character, too. A good foil."

"A good foil?"

"Yes, I mean, for my character. This man was amazing. I pulled a bunch of stuff about him off the internet. There's a big pile of it in my suitcase. I haven't had a chance to read it all, but it looks fantastic. You're going to love him."

"I'll read the script, and judge for myself," said Tom.

"I tell you, Tom, it's going to blow your mind. I can't wait to see what you think. You must read it tonight."

"I will. I can read it after we have supper. You can get some rest —"

"No, no, no! I want to go out. Let's go somewhere lively. I'm sure you know a good bar. We can get a few good belts inside us, and you can read it while we're drinking."

"Are you sure you wouldn't rather stay home and get some rest?"

"Rest? Who needs that? No, we are going on the town!"

"Sean, do you think it's wise to be discussing alchemy and witchcraft in a public place? People at nearby tables will think we're raving fruitcakes."

"Who cares? Let the peasants think what they will. Take me to yonder tavern, Sirrah. I command thee!"

~

The Economy Shoe Shop was not especially crowded, so Sean and Tom received frequent and prompt attention from the staff at their table in the back corner. They were both drinking steadily, but whereas Tom was downing about one glass of beer per half hour, Sean was drinking more often and was taking whisky chasers with his beer.

One of the waitresses recognized Sean, and the way some people at other tables were sneaking glances at him suggested that they had, too. This pleased Sean immensely, and he leant back in his chair, surveying the bar as if he owned the place.

Meanwhile, Tom was studiously reading the script, taking extra care to try to absorb what he saw in the pages. Eventually, he reached the end, and deliberately placed the script on the table. He was still wearing his reading glasses, but his eyes were unfocused as he stared thoughtfully into space.

Sean turned back from examining the room and, seeing the closed script, was expectant, almost fearful. "So?"

"Hmm."

"What do you think?"

"You're right, it is...remarkable. It's very different. I don't think

I've read a script like it."

"And…?"

"It's also kind of unsettling."

"Yeah. Well, it's about weird stuff which is bound to set your mind going in a thousand different directions. But you like it?"

"Yes," said Tom. "I guess I like it well enough."

"Good. I mean what a man! He wrote something like eighty books on mathematics, science, geography, navigation, ciphers, chemistry, religion, and God knows what else."

"A learned man, for sure."

"You can say that again. He studied at London, Paris, Cambridge, Louvain—wherever that is—"

"Belgium, I think."

"Belgium? Okay. Guy must have had a huge intellect."

"And yet he believed he could turn lead into gold, talk to the dead and see the future in a crystal ball."

"Maybe he could. How do we know?"

"Oh, come on!"

"Alright, but maybe it's possible. We don't know everything. What arrogance to think that the twenty-first century has all the answers. Maybe those old guys knew things that have since been forgotten."

"How many drinks have you had?

"A few. Why? You backing out? Are you getting cold feet?"

"I don't know. I'm not sure."

"What's your problem?"

"I don't know if I have a problem. It's just that there's something not quite right about all this. I can't put my finger on it, but I'm uneasy in my gut."

"You're nuts. Don't fuck me around. Don't betray me."

"No, I won't betray you. That's a weird way of putting it."

"And you'll do it? With me?"

"Yeah. I think. Okay, you talked me into it. You're on."

Sean let out a whoop, reached over and gave an embarrassed Tom a sloppy hug. Sean could smell the whisky on his breath and wondered how many he had put away.

Over Tom's shoulder, Sean noticed a good looking, red-haired, young woman at a distant table. She wore a white tee-shirt and jeans, and had her hair pinned up. When Sean yelled she looked over at him. He gave her a little wave, but she ignored it and returned to her conversation with two other young people.

Sean released Tom from the clumsy embrace and ordered more drinks. "Welcome aboard, old buddy. Now, listen: here's the plan. First plane we can get, we're out of here."

"To England?"

"Yes, of course to England! I already explained to you, we need to go over to do research, to get into his head. We need to visit all the places where he lived."

"All the places? You're kidding. How many are there?"

"I don't know, but it will be easy enough to find out! I want you to be serious about this, for God's sake! We need to soak up the atmosphere. We can do a bit of location scouting at the same time. Sollows seems like an amenable sort of guy. After all, he took you on sight unseen."

Sean guffawed at his own witticism, but Tom looked thoughtful and did not immediately respond.

"What's up? You don't want to go? Come on. We'll have a ball!"

"Okay, I'll go. I guess it can't do any harm to go take a look. You talked me into it."

IX

It was a blustery day in the ancient seaside town of Hastings, and the many ships in port were clapping against the wet wood of the wharfings. Boarding or disembarking from any of them was a precarious pursuit and, indeed, an unfortunate fellow had recently lost his balance, slipped between boat and wharf, and had been crushed. Such like accidents happened several times a year when the weather was blowy; days when few men might keep their hats without tying them down.

But weather cannot step in the way of commerce and, despite the gale, the waterfront was busy with men scurrying to and fro, anxious to complete their business afore the turn of the tide. The quay was accordingly cluttered with boxes, bags, bales, sacks, barrels, baskets, carts, rope coils, and fish bins.

Balanced on the very edge of the dock, behind a stack of large cases, was Dr. Dee, his black cloak wildly flapping about him. The doctor was in deep, but subdued lest others should hear, discussion with a sea captain. This ship's master, Will Rolls, was a man of advanced years who was no stranger to foreign parts, having visited Spain, Italy and Poland in his time, and would again by the next tide be bound for Gdansk.

Some coins changed hands and the captain nodded his assent to the task with which he had been charged.

~

In the Sussex town of Folkstown, the next day, in a dark and smoky corner of a raucous, crowded inn. Dr. Dee was ensconced with one Jem Starkey, a customs official for Her Majesty's Treasury. This was a dank, but commodious tavern, much frequented by the common people.

Starkey spoke in whispers, so the doctor had to lean almost full across the table to hear the man. As the fellow spoke, the doctor made notes in a small pocketbook.

Then he placed several silver groats under the fellow's tankard.

~

The day following that, Dr. Dee was in the old market town of Horsham. The day was fine, as befits Market Day, and the citizens were abroad in large numbers. The square was bursting with carts, wagons and stalls, selling all manner of provender and merchandise.

The bustle and babble were almost deafening as the cries of the hawkers mingled with the incessant chatter of customers. These in turn competed with the lowing and bellowing of cattle, the squeal of pigs, the bleating of lambs, and the clucking of hens. Joining the chorus was the clattering of pots and pans, the clanging of the blacksmith and the tap-tapping of the tinsmith.

One large stall was loaded high with earthenware and other forms of pottery, together with a little china for the wealthier classes. The most numerous items for sale were solid, blue and grey Westerweld stoneware jugs and tankards, and beautiful blue and white Delft plates and vessels.

Dr. Dee came hither not to purchase any of these fine things, but to converse with the German who owned the stall. Speaking to the fellow in his own tongue, the doctor outlined what he wished him to accomplish on his travels back to his home in the Rheinland Palatinate.

Jobst Hallfrizscht, for that was his name, nodded in agreement and gladly took the sixpences from the doctor's hand.

~

The next morning shone bright and clear and found the good doctor busy in the pursuit of writing letters. Several, which were completed and ready for dispatch, lay at hand. Two were in the German language, two in Spanish, one in Polish, another in Magyar. A small candle burned in its holder, alongside a number of sticks of sealing wax.

He finished writing, then rang a little bell which sat on the desk.

Dr. Dee's steward and amanuensis, Edward Talbot, who sometimes called himself Kelley, entered upon the sound of the bell. Talbot was a young, sallow-complexioned man of twenty-seven summers, with shifty, dark eyes and a sour expression. He wore a long, brown robe, a chain of office on which hung many keys, and a tightly-fitting, black skull cap. From closer examination of this cap, it transpired that the wearer had no external ears.

When he spoke, Talbot did so in a bucolic, Worcestershire accent, which was always subservient and meek when addressing his master, but hard and cruel when attending to those of lesser rank. Talbot stood behind the doctor's chair while he folded, addressed and sealed the letters.

Dr. Dee then placed them in a canvas bag which he handed to his servant. "Have the groom take these to Portsmouth immediately. I want them to catch tomorrow morning's tide."

"Certainly, doctor."

When the steward had departed with the correspondence, Dr. Dee stroked his beard thoughtfully, as if he were wrestling with a decision he would rather indefinitely postpone.

10

The day after Sean's arrival in Halifax, Tom let him sleep well into the morning. He went out and about on a few errands, and when he returned Sean was still wrapped in a blanket on the couch, snoring loudly.

It was not until past eleven that Tom decided that it was time Sean should be stirring, and made coffee. He carried a mug into the living room and poked Sean with his foot. "Rise and shine, Dr. Dee. 'Tis I, your humble servant with a restorative libation."

"Oh hello, Tom." Sean swung his feet on to the floor, yawned and gratefully accepted the coffee.

"How are you feeling?"

"A little frayed around the edges. I read the script again after you went to bed."

"Jesus! I don't know how you could make sense of it. You were pissed out of your skull. Are you sure you're alright?"

"I'm fine. Just a little tired, that's all."

"I'm not so sure you are fine, Sean. I know you've always been a heavy drinker, and you had a shit load last night, but there's something else going on here."

"What are you talking about?"

"Look, you've worked on—what is it?—some sixty-five scripts, but this one seems to be doing some kind of number on you."

"You're nuts!" Sean said resentfully, "Sure, I'm getting caught up in it. That's because it's the best one I've ever seen. So what do you expect?"

"It's just that you don't seem yourself. At least not the way I've known you all these years."

Nursing his coffee, Sean rose and walked to the window. He looked out at the harbour for a few minutes, then turned back to Tom. "Okay, I'll tell you. It's Liz. She's left me. Just walked out. When I woke up the other day she was gone."

"Ah. I'm sorry to hear that, Sean. I liked Liz. I thought you and she were solid."

"She gave me a whole bunch of bullshit about my lifestyle and how our relationship was unnatural. Unnatural! I think she wanted me to become an insurance salesman, get a house in the suburbs and join the local bridge club."

"It may be the old story about the clock ticking. She probably wanted to get married and settle down. Have kids."

"I would marry her, for Christ's sake, but do I have to become a monk? I treated her well, but she never gave me the credit I deserve. She automatically assumed the worst about me. About what I think, what my motives are, what I feel. I know my faults, and I've got lots of them, but I deserve better than this."

"Any chance of mending things?"

"She says we'll talk when we get back from England."

"That means there's still hope. I don't mind telling you that I've had mixed feelings about this trip. But maybe it's a good thing after all. You can let the dust settle, do some thinking. Figure out your priorities..."

"Did you make the flight reservations?"

"Not yet. I needed to check with you first. If we want to get away in the next three days, we have to go in Business Class."

"That's not a problem."

"It's much more expensive."

"Just do it, Tom. See if we can get out tonight. If not, then tomorrow night."

~

They were able to secure tickets for that night, and later Sean and Tom were walking past the hundreds of passengers waiting on the departure level at Stanfield International as they headed for the Maple Leaf Lounge. Sean had already had a few drinks, but was in a reasonably quiet, if febrile state.

Tom was idly scanning the mass of travellers when he noticed a heavenly young woman studying the departures monitor. Stunned by her beauty, he grabbed Sean by the arm. "Look Sean! My God, what a gorgeous woman."

"Too young for you, Tom. You're probably old enough to be her much older brother. I wonder who she is. She looks familiar. I've seen her around somewhere. You know her?"

"Me?" Tom sighed. "No. I wish I did."

They checked into the Business Class lounge, where they obtained some drinks.

"To the women we can never have," Sean said, raising his class.

~

Sean and Tom were comfortably seated near the nose of the aircraft. Several of the flight attendants were whispering together and glancing in Sean's direction. They had seen some of his films and were commenting on how much younger he appeared in the flesh. One of the attendants served them Champagne and canapes, and the two friends were enjoying the sense of envied luxury as the economy passengers struggled past them.

Tom averted his eyes from these travellers, as their resentment was palpable, and turned his attention to Sean's recitation of more of Dr. Dee's accomplishments. "I wouldn't mind re-discovering the formula to turn lead into gold," he said.

"Wouldn't that be something? What if they really did it and their formula still exists?"

"Guarded by blind monks in a monastery high in the remote mountains of Wales?"

"Fuck yes! Wouldn't that be wild?" Sean cackled.

Once they were airborne and the seat-belt light had been turned off, they became aware of one of the attendants.

"Excuse me, sir, but there's a young lady from Economy Class who would like a word with you. I told her I couldn't allow it without your permission."

"She's probably a fan," said Sean. "Okay, let her come in."

The attendant retreated behind the curtain separating the Economy and Business sections.

"I'm sorry to bother you, but aren't you Sean Dorch?" a soft voice asked.

Sean and Tom swivelled around to see who was addressing them. Tom's heart almost missed several beats. He gaped at this amazing vision. It was the woman he had seen earlier.

"Yes, I'm Sean Dorch."

"Mr. Dorch, I wondered if I could get your autograph."

"Sure," Sean said, taking her note book and scribbling in it.

"I'm sorry, Miss," interrupted the attendant, bristling with petty authority, "but you'll have to return to your own cabin."

"That's alright. She's only staying a couple of minutes."

"If you say so, Mr. Dorch, but not too long. Otherwise we could get all kinds of people trooping into the Business Section."

"I saw you at the Economy Shoe Shop last night," said the young woman once the attendant had disappeared.

"Ah! I thought I knew from somewhere. Are you on vacation?"

"Yes, I just graduated from theatre school, so I'm giving myself a treat."

"Hey. We're all in the same business," said Sean. "You hear that, Tom? This is my friend Tom Johnson. He's an actor too."

"I know," she said, and to Tom she added: "I've seen quite a lot of your stuff."

"Hello." The word stuck in his throat and came out as a hoarse whisper. He could not stop himself from staring at her in a totally besotted manner.

"So, are you visiting family in the old country?" Sean asked.

"No, I don't know anyone there. I'm just going to bum around. Hitchhiking. I'll go wherever I can get rides, I guess."

The attendant was on the move again, not looking pleased.

"I'd better go before I get everybody into trouble."

"What's your name?" Tom asked, infatuated.

"Tamsin."

She disappeared. The attendant adjusted the curtain and returned to the front of the cabin.

"Tamsin," Tom said quietly to himself.

XI

Tomos was observing his cousin at work one day in one of the doctor's workshops. On the bench was a small brazier in which the doctor, by means of a long pair of iron tongs, was melting some substance in a crucible. As he worked, he referred to extensive notes which were spread out upon the table top on his left-hand side. Several times he added drops of liquid from a ceramic bottle.

Tomos watched this from a distance, although from time to time he came closer in order to peer over the doctor's shoulder. "Shall I disturb your work if I converse with you?"

"By no means. I have performed this experiment many times before."

"Thomasina tells me that you are reputed to have met three monarchs of the realm in the face. I'm impressed, cousin. In Wales, I do not believe we have seen any monarchs, at least not in this century."

"You have been speaking with Thomasina?"

"I exchange a little conversation with her when I see her about the house in the execution of her duties."

"I see," said Dr. Dee somewhat coldly. "Yes, I met the young King Edward in, I think, 1551, and four years later I met Queen Mary. Queen Elizabeth I have met a number of times. At her palaces and at my house."

"She came to your home?" Tomos was surprised by this news.

"The first time Her Majesty graced my house was in 1574. It was both sad and uplifting, and revealed how gracious she can be."

"In what manner?"

"The day before her visit, my wife—my previous wife, before Jane —went to God, and when the Queen came she had been buried but four hours. She grieved to hear that Mrs. Dee had passed on and confessed herself deeply touched that I had not sought to cancel the visit on that account.

"But out of respect for my wife's memory and my own feelings, she refused to enter a house of mourning, instead entreating me to entertain and instruct her in the forecourt. She especially wished to see my renowned magic glass, so I sent for it at once, and imparted to her my understanding of its powers."

Tomos regarded his cousin seriously, wondering if such fantastic events could be true.

The doctor withdrew the crucible from the flames and poured its contents into a small mould. The molten, yellow metal gleamed brightly as it ran from the crucible's lip.

On seeing this, Tomos let out a gasp, imagining he saw gold.

Before he could question his cousin, the doctor continued his tale. "The Queen came again just a few years ago, desiring me to explain the extent and nature of her title to lands discovered in the New World."

"This time she came inside the house?"

"Yes. She was within for many hours."

An unpleasant sound of throat clearing alerted them to Talbot's silent approach.

"Ah, Talbot. What is it?"

"Dispatches from the Continent, Master."

"Excellent. Leave them on the bench."

Talbot did as he was bade and padded out of the workshop. Dr.

Dee opened the pouch which Talbot had brought, and hungrily started to read.

"Forgive me for being free with my opinions, cousin, but I do not like that man," said Tomos with great feeling.

"This is promising," said the doctor. "My contact in Madrid indicates that he may soon have something of great interest for me. What was that you said just now?"

"I spoke of Talbot. I said I did not like the fellow. I wonder you could employ a man like that, let alone confide in him."

"He serves his purposes."

"That cap he wears is so tight it is inconceivable that the man has any ears underneath."

"He does not. He had them cut off at Lancaster when he was in the pillory."

"In the pillory!?"

"The poor fellow was convicted of forgery. The Lancaster magistrates were lenient. I have heard of some who lost hands and testicles for similar offences."

"Yet, knowing all this, you employed him?" Tomos could not understand it.

"The fellow has many faults, no doubt, but I need him. He is the only one who can see the visions in the crystal. The angels speak to me through him. He is my skryer."

Tomos was taken aback by this information, and was incredulous. He shifted nervously. "The angels?"

"Yes. The messages they bring assist me in seeing into the future. Two in particular—Aneal and Uriel—are of immense value to me in interpreting the many matters which are brought before me."

Tomos was staggered by what he had heard and was flustered. "Forgive me. I had no idea he was so important to you."

Dr. Dee paused as if regretting an indiscretion, collected himself, and addressed Tomos directly. "And what reasons, pray, do you have to dislike the man?"

"I do not trust him. He seems devious and sly. And I do not like the way he looks at Thomasina. It is obvious she fears him greatly."

"Ah. Now we come to the real matter. You fear him because you yourself have similar designs upon the maid."

"Upon my word, cousin," retorted Tomos in embarrassment, "I know not what you mean."

"Do you not? Well, we shall see. Meantime, do not think of my dismissing Talbot. He is indispensable."

~

That evening, the setting sun suffused the garden shrubs and hedges with an unreal, roseate glow as Thomasina collected the laundry she had previously hung out to dry on lines strung between the old apple trees. She wore her long skirts tucked up to avoid them catching on the uncut grass, and carried a large basket over one pink arm.

Tomos came round the corner of the house and, casting about to ensure that nobody else was around, quietly approached her. When she heard his footfall swishing through the sward, she turned, startled.

"Forgive me for coming upon you unawares, Thomasina."

"'Tis alright, Master Tomos. I feared 'twas that fellow Talbot creeping up on me again. The fellow makes my flesh crawl."

Unknown to Thomasina and Tomos, Dr. Dee was observing them through a small basement window.

"It is partly about Talbot that I wished to speak with you in private. Do his attentions trouble you?"

"Indeed they do, though there is little I can do about it. He is the Steward and I am but a serving maid."

"I understand. I want you to know that if he should…you know…extend his attentions to the point of making free with your person, you must not hesitate to call upon me immediately for assistance."

"That is most kind of you, sir. It sets my mind more at ease."

Tomos made as if to go, hesitated, and then turned back to her. He glanced around the garden again before speaking. "Thomasina, while I greatly enjoy our little talks together, it might be wiser if we held them only when we are sure we are alone."

"Sir?"

"Otherwise, I think it might serve to provoke Talbot and we must avoid that for your protection. Also, I think your master disapproves of my befriending you."

"Why should he do that, sir?"

"I will be blunt with you. In short, he guesses that I have formed an attachment to you."

Thomasina blushed, but looked him straight in the eye. "Does he guess aright, sir?"

"I fear he does," said Tomos, acutely embarrassed. "I have become exceeding fond of you, Thomasina. Given the many years between our ages I know I can never expect my feelings to be returned."

"Then you would be wrong, sir. You are not old, and as good a figure of a man as any I can see anywhere in these parts."

"How kind you are! You have brought happiness to my day. We shall speak of this again soon. I must go now or they will be wondering what has been keeping you so long."

Tomos walked back through the orchard, his step livelier than when he came.

At his window, Dr. Dee watched him go as Thomasina collected the last of the laundry. As he was about to return to his work, Dee spied another figure lurking in the distance behind some bushes.

When at length the figure emerged, he saw that it was Talbot.

12

The remainder of their flight was uneventful. Tom managed to get a little more than five hours sleep, but Sean stayed awake re-reading the script and drinking.

The plane arrived at Heathrow on time and, impatient and tired, the friends moved slowly in the long line of passengers through Immigration. Although their Business Class tickets allowed them to use the fast lane, it was still a lengthy process.

While Sean was scribbling notes in the margins of the script, Tom unsuccessfully scanned the other travellers, hoping to catch a glimpse of Tamsin.

They had to wait for about fifteen minutes outside the terminal for the Hertz bus to take them to the car hire station. It was a typical grey and cloudy early morning in Britain, but a faint pinprick of sunlight in the far-distant sky promised the possibility of some fine weather later in the day.

The bright yellow bus arrived and they clambered on board. There were only four other travellers, none of them of particular interest to Tom, who was still disappointed at not seeing Tamsin again; nor to Sean, who still had his head stuck in the script.

At the Hertz office on the airport's Northern Perimeter Road, they presented their reservation information together with their drivers' licenses, and received the keys and the paperwork. They were surprised to learn that most insurance packages did not provide coverage for theft of the vehicle, so Sean insisted on getting the Super Cover which protected them against all eventualities without there being any deductible.

A very obliging sales clerk escorted them to the vast parking lot filled with shiny cars, took them to a large white sedan, and explained how they could negotiate the numerous roads in order to exit the airport. Tom took a wrong turn anyway, so it took them at least twenty minutes before they could get out of the huge airport complex and onto the M4 motorway.

It was the first time Tom had driven in the metropolitan London area, and the extremely heavy traffic and confusing signposting were causing him considerable difficulty. No sooner was he on the M4 than he had to negotiate an elaborate "spaghetti" junction and turn-off onto another motorway, the M25. Cars were whizzing past him at high speeds.

His nerves already frayed, when he saw a Burger King on the outskirts of Egham, he pulled off and into the parking lot.

"What's your problem?" Sean demanded. "You want to eat already?"

"I need to take a breath. This road system is insane."

"Pull yourself together, Tom. We have places to go, things to see."

"You want to drive?" Tom was testy.

"No, no. Do what you have to do."

"Well, I need to check the map before I do anything else. Then I want to figure out a plan. This flying blind will do us no good."

"Alright. Go ahead."

Tom opened the road atlas they had bought at the airport bookstore and studied it for what seemed to Sean was an eternity. Then he scratched a few notes on the inside of the cover.

"You ready yet?" Sean asked.

"Yes, I think so. So, I've got a plan. Want to hear it?"

"You're the navigator."

"Okay. We want to go to Hampton Court and Mortlake. Right?"

"Right."

"So we go down this motorway and then left on the M3, then right on the A308 at a place called Sunbury on Thames. That should take us to Hampton Court."

"Good!"

"Between there and Mortlake is Kingston upon Thames—"

"I won't ask if these places are near the river."

"Funny guy! So, when we've seen Hampton Court, I think we should find a hotel in Kingston and rest there today. Tomorrow we'll go to Mortlake. That's alright?"

"Sounds good. But somewhere we must get a pub lunch!"

"I thought you'd say that. There's a pub called The Black Horse in Kingston."

"Excellent!"

"And for good measure, I propose we stay at the White Hart Hotel tonight."

"Okay."

"This is where you have to do some work. Get on your phone and find the hotel, get its number and then call and make reservations."

~

After several more wrong turns and driving round in circles, they eventually reached Hampton Court, the famous out-of-town residence of King Henry VIII, and one of only two of his palaces still standing. It was originally built by Cardinal Wolsey in 1514 but he gave it to the king as a bribe some fifteen years later. It is likely that the gift prevented his being beheaded, but Wolsey only lived another year, dying in misery in 1530 on his way from York to London.

Beyond getting to the palace, Sean and Tom really had no itemized plan since they did not really know what they were looking for, and later that morning saw them wandering around the courtyard.

Suddenly, Sean cried out, stumbled and fell down. As Tom helped him up, Sean grabbed his arm. "This is where they seized him, Tom. Right here is where they took him to prison. I had a vision. There's no doubt about it. And they dragged him…"

Looking around, Sean spied a gate in the wall. He pointed to it excitedly. "…there. They took him through there!"

Sean went up to the gate, which was securely locked. He ran his hands over the wrought iron work, and then took pictures with his phone. Tom stood, staring and wondering.

After drifting through the state rooms, examining suits of armour and portraits, they went through the allegedly-haunted gallery and wound up in the great hall with its magnificent oak hammer beam roof and rich wall tapestries. Sean said he had received slight indications of Dr. Dee's presence in the latter, but not the former.

Tom shook his head, asking himself how anyone could make themselves known after some four hundred and fifty years.

The Black Horse was not quite the rustic old pub that Tom had envisioned, but it was a comfortable establishment with wood panelling and many framed prints on the walls. Sean had the fish and chips while Tom chose the Pie of the Day, which turned out to be steak and kidney and was very tasty. Tom had a pint and a half of St. Austell's Virtue beer, but Sean, somewhat ominously, decided on two pints of Doom Bar ale.

By now, both friends were jet-lagged and a little inebriated, so they drove back through Kingston, over the river to the White Hart in Hampton Wick. The hotel was a pleasant-looking place in an artificial half-timbered and red-brick style. Inside it was very welcoming in a smart, warm, mainly brown décor with leather arm chairs and benches.

Their rooms were beautifully appointed, Sean securing the larger of the two which had a big print of the river in times gone by. Here, they slept until dinner time.

After showering, they both felt restored and met in the lounge for drinks. Seated under a mounted stag's head, they reclined in the commodious chairs, and decided to whet their appetites with a bottle of English Bolney sparkling wine, which the waiter informed them came from Sussex.

At this mention, Sean nudged Tom and whispered, "Sussex. Dr. Dee country."

To start their dinner, they decided to share the hummus and roast red pepper dip with tzatziki, marinated olives and grilled pitta breads. Then Sean ordered the fish and prawn pie, while Tom had the roast chicken.

In rather ostentatious fashion, Sean asked for a bottle of Puligny-Montrachet, insisting that it be served not too cold. On being told the white wines were kept in a fridge, he asked for it to be brought to the table immediately and be allowed to come to just under room temperature.

They did not linger after dinner, still being jet-lagged, so went to bed immediately.

Some ten hours later, well rested, they returned to the same table and devoured an enormous breakfast of fried eggs, pork sausage, bacon, Hampshire black pudding, grilled tomatoes, field mushrooms, hash browns, and baked beans. This they washed down with many cups of Americano coffee.

Although it was only seven miles away, due to several more wrong turnings, they did not reach Mortlake until early in the afternoon. With some difficulty they found a parking space, and idly sauntered along by the river.

"You know what?" Sean said. "I feel him. I feel his presence here."

"Sean, there's nothing here that I can see which is over four hundred years old. Besides, didn't you tell me that his place was burned down by the mob?"

"Burned yes, but not down. The records show that, not long after the fire, he was still living somewhere around here. That means that either he was able to repair the place or he got another house in the vicinity."

As they moved in the direction of the church, they saw a middle-aged woman coming towards them.

"Excuse me ma'am, can you tell us if the house of Dr. John Dee is anywhere around here?"

"Who?"

"The famous Dr. John Dee."

"I don't know him. There's a clinic in Richmond. You might find him there. Is he the gynecologist?"

Tom turned away, helpless with laughter.

"Thank you for your time, ma'am," said Sean.

Puzzled, the woman walked down the path.

Tom was holding onto a lamp post for support. "Add it to the list, Sean. Dr. Dee, famous black magician, astrologer, and gynecologist! Maybe he did obstetrics, too!"

Sean was clearly annoyed. "Come on. This is serious research we're talking about."

Tom was still sniggering as they walked further.

Suddenly, Sean stopped and stared in the direction of the river. "Laugh if you like, but I know he was here. Somewhere very close by."

"Maybe he was a back street abortionist!" Tom guffawed.

Sean shot him a dirty look and stalked away. Tom followed him at a distance.

At length they came to the Church of St. Mary the Virgin and went inside. When Sean opened the heavy oak door there was a loud, almost thunderous, echo.

The musty church was hushed and cold, and eerie beams of light streamed through the stained glass windows. Their footsteps on the flagstones reverberated strangely.

"You know anything about churches?" Sean asked.

"A fair amount."

"This is the nave, right?"

"Yes. The main body of the church is the nave. Right."

"And that part at the end—where the altar is—what's that?"

"That would be the chancel."

"Alright. Follow me!"

They walked the full length of the church until they were in the apse. Sean swept the area with his eyes and suddenly grabbed Tom's arm.

"There! You can't argue with that," he said triumphantly.

Following his pointing finger, Tom saw, set in the floor, a black plaque. They looked in silence while Sean took pictures with his phone.

Near this place lie the remains of
JOHN DEE MA
CLERK IN HOLY ORDERS
1527-1609
Astronomer, Geographer
Mathematician
Adviser to Queen Elizabeth I

"Now you can't say he wasn't here!" Sean was exultant.

"He was here, alright. I wonder how much of him is left wherever they buried him. Maybe we should come back under cover of darkness and dig for his bones."

Sean was not amused by Tom's foolery and roughly pushed him towards the exit.

Halfway down the aisle, Tom stopped. "Maybe he was never here, Sean. Maybe they buried a fake. Maybe the real Dee's body was taken to a remote monastery in the Welsh mountains."

"Guarded by blind monks, no doubt," said Sean acidly.

"Of course."

"Fuck off!"

"Sean, it's a mortal sin to swear in church."

Sean pushed him forward more forcibly and propelled him through the door. "I don't know why I wanted to bring you on this trip. So far, you've just been a pain in the ass!"

~

Later that night, back at the hotel, Sean decided to call Liz. He sat on the bed surrounded by the script and his many notes. Since her time zone was four hours behind his, he figured she would just be getting home from work.

"I'm glad you are having a good time, Sean, but I really don't want to talk to you. I don't want to go over it again. It's still much too soon."

"I miss you, Liz. I still need you. You don't believe me, do you? You never thought I was good enough for you."

"No, Sean. Right about now I don't think you're good enough for me. I've just got in from the office and I have things to do."

"Liz, just listen to me—"

"Goodbye, Sean."

When the phone rang again, Liz ignored it and went about preparing her evening meal.

XIII

It was a perfect night with no clouds in a sky, which was brilliantly punctuated by myriad stars and a clear, yellow moon. The wind, which had earlier in the day lashed the downs, had dissipated, and all was now still. Only the occasional sound of nocturnal creatures intruded upon the peaceful scene.

Close to each other, but not touching, Tomos and Thomasina were strolling slowly along. They were in sight, but not within earshot, of the manor.

"So, that is all there is to know about me, Thomasina. I am a very ordinary man who usually stays at his farm in Radnorshire. I visit my cousin exceedingly seldom, and came to be invited on this occasion only because your master had learned of my modest studies on rock formations and the properties of different kinds of stone."

"You are very clever, sir, I am sure of that."

"No, not I. Your master is a clever man. For all his faults and foibles, he is a brilliant man who is renowned throughout all Europe for his accomplishments. By the by, Thomasina, you must not address me as "sir". Not when we are alone. You know my name."

"I do, sir. It is Tomos. It is an unusual name, at least in these parts."

"It is a Welsh name. Some say it is a form of 'Thomas'. As, I think, is your own name, which I think comes from the ancient Aramaic language."

"I did not know its origin, sir…Tomos…but I was named for my father who is indeed called Thomas."

"So we are linked by our names."

"Sir…Tomos…did you ever wed?"

"No, but I will not say it was because I never found the right woman. There was a girl once—many years ago—whom I loved and would have gladly wed, but she was joined with another by her family. He was a man of much greater rank and property than I, and much more to her father's liking. As I say, that was a long time ago and, alas, I have heard that she has since died."

"That is very sad, sir."

"Tomos."

"Forgive me. Tomos. Your story brought tears to my eyes."

"I wonder how many others could tell a similar tale. Many thousands. I fear what we call love plays little part in most marriages. Largely, it is a matter of money, connections, or rank. Or convenience."

"I believe that is true, Tomos."

"But what I feel for you has naught to do with any of those considerations. Since my unfortunate attachment all those years ago, I have not felt the same about anyone. I freely confess that I love you."

"No man has ever spoken to me like this before."

Tomos sat down on a large boulder, bidding Thomasina to join him. He immediately felt the warmth of her body as she leaned against him. They sat silently, gazing into the glittering firmament.

"I have alluded to the difference between our ages. But if you were able to put that aside, you might do a deal worse. You would be mistress of a property of some one hundred and twenty hides of land, much of it quite productive, and a good household with your own servants."

"Oh, Tomos!"

"I have not told you the best. Your abode would be in the beautiful countryside. These downs are good, but they cannot compare with the woods, hills and fields around Llanbister, where I hail from."

"Tomos. I am greatly honoured by what you have said. Am I to understand that you are asking for my hand?"

"God's death, what a fool I am! I have not put the question! May I do so now? Will you wed me, Thomasina?"

"I will think on it and will, of course, consult my father. But it is only fair to tell you, Tomos, that I am looking very kindly upon your offer."

"It makes me very happy to hear you speak thus. When you do, it is like the sun shining into my soul. But we should make haste. You have been gone from the house too long."

As they rose and moved aroint towards the manor, they did not notice the dark figure of Talbot lurking behind some nearby bushes, but they did see Dr. Dee standing at some distance on the crest of the downs. He was studying the heavens with a strange instrument.

"We must part company. Go you around by the orchard and in by the back way. I will approach my cousin as if I had come upon him when walking by myself."

"It shall be so, Tomos. But before I go shall you not leave me with some small remembrance?"

"Indeed I shall."

Tomos took her in his arms and gently kissed her. Thomasina separated from him and hurried away.

Tomos walked onward towards the black robed figure silhouetted against the shimmering sky. "Cousin! How now? You could not have chosen a better night to study the stars."

"Indeed not. I knew not that you were abroad tonight."

"I was just taking the air when I observed your activity."

Dr. Dee regarded him somewhat suspiciously and returned to his observations.

Just then, Tomos noticed a falling star. "Is that a comet, cousin?"

"No, no. Nothing of the kind, It is merely a star which has lost its way. Let us walk and I will tell you about comets."

They wandered along the tops of the downs, surrounded by millions of pinpoints of light. Tomos thought it was an awesome and humbling experience to be privileged to see such a sight.

"'Twas in the year 1577 when I was sent for by the Queen concerning the Great Comet. I heard what commotions went on at court from Devereux who was present at the time.

"A soon as the comet appeared, the whole court was thrown into confusion, this one saying the comet bode ill for Her Majesty's health, that one opining that the crops would fail, another that a plague would descend upon the land.

"Apparently, the Queen shouted, 'Enough!' and said they were chattering like peasants or children at their mother's knee. She said that none of them knew what the marvel portended and that they should send to Mortlake for myself. According to Devereux, the Queen said, 'Let him come to me. If there be any man in Christendom who knows what this comet means, it is John Dee.'"

"That is indeed very remarkable," said Tomos, obviously impressed.

"I attended Her Majesty and, for three days, she kept me by her side, begging for explanations and speculations. At her insistence, I gave such a lengthy dissertation that the subject was entirely exhausted. Naturally, I was able to set the Queen's mind at rest and she was much gratified and relieved."

"I am sure Her Majesty was extremely grateful to you."

"Strange you should say that, Tomos. You might think that she would shower me with gifts."

"She did not?"

"Marry, she did not! She gave me no reward for my services beyond promises. If I could have banked her promises, I would be as rich as Croesus."

"That was not right, cousin," Tomos said. "Were you able to discern the reason for this ingratitude?"

"I believe I did not get my just desserts from the Queen because the Court despised me for what they see as my humble birth. You will be aware that my father was tailor to King Henry. But the fools did not know that I am one of the Ddus of Nant y Groes in Radnorshire and am a direct descendant of Rhodri Mawr the Prince of Wales."

"Indeed, the world is a most unjust place." Tomos observed gravely as they turned back towards the house.

14

On leaving Kingston upon Thames, they decided not to go back on motorways because the speed of the traffic made Tom nervous, and since it was clear Sean had no intention of driving, the decision was not debated.

With great difficulty, they eventually found their way on to the A303 heading west, with the object of reaching Stonehenge. Almost inevitably, Tom had become lost in the Kingston suburbs and had, by accident not design, found the A3, which tediously took them through the built-up areas of Guildford and Farnham, which in turn meant heavy traffic congestion and considerable loss of time.

At Farnham, Tom found himself on the A31, which took them south, in the wrong direction, to Winchester where, hours behind their schedule, they decided to have lunch.

His nerves frayed to the limit, Tom was approaching the River Itchen when, on the other bank, they saw a pub called The Bishop on the Bridge. He crossed over the river and parked the car in the first space he could see, past caring whether or not he was in a restricted zone. They both had burgers and pints of London Pride.

"Winchester is an ancient city," said Sean, "I wonder if Dr. Dee came here?"

"He might have, at one time or another."

"Let me look at my notes."

"Don't let your burger get cold."

"Here it is." Sean gave Tom a cold look. "I can't place him in Winchester, but one of his protégés, a Dr. Meric Casaubon, founded a school here. Anyway, there's a medieval cathedral, and Alfred the Great is supposed to have come from here. I think the cathedral warrants a decent visit."

"I always liked that song, *Winchester Cathedral*. Was that the New Vaudeville Band?"

"Oh yes, I remember. We must see the cathedral. The Winchester Bible is very famous, having been written in the twelfth century. And I hear they say there are twelve kings buried there. My notes also tell me that Jane Austen is interred in the cathedral."

"Sean, if we do that we might not be able to see Stonehenge, Avebury and Durrington Walls, all of which you wanted to take in today."

"Hmm. Tell you what, Tom. Let's take a peek at the cathedral, then do Stonehenge later this afternoon. If we can find a hotel in the vicinity, we can do those other places tomorrow before we head off to Glastonbury."

"Okay, if that's what you want. But bear in mind that, with these crazy roads and this insane traffic, it's impossible to judge arrival times."

"I understand. Where do we have to go to get back on track when we leave here?"

Tom opened the road atlas and pored over it for several minutes, scribbling notes from time to time. He finished his beer and wiped the froth from his mouth.

"Okay. Assuming we can get out of the city, we have to go back north on the A34 to the A303 which should take us directly to Stonehenge."

"Good." Sean was on his phone, looking up accommodations. "Ah! Here's one. The New Inn just outside Avebury. That would be perfect. I'll book it."

They got lost again, foolishly trying to reach the A34 by driving through the city, and ended up in a village called Littleton. From there Tom managed to find their way, and headed north until they reached the westward road at Lower Bullington. It was now well into the afternoon, but although the traffic was heavy, it was relatively well paced.

They recovered their spirits and, as they sped along, they ran lines from the script.

When they were just past Amesbury, Tom noticed a girl hitch-hiker waving her thumb in the air. They were a hundred yards past the girl before Tom realized that it was Tamsin.

He stepped on the brakes and swerved the car to the side of the road as other motorists furiously blew their horns and made crude gestures.

"What the hell!" Sean shouted. "You're creating a traffic jam. Why are we stopping?

"It's Tamsin," said Tom, delighted. "She needs a ride."

Seeing their car had stopped, Tamsin hastily ran along the grass verge and, breathless and smiling, tumbled into the back seat, dragging her rucksack behind her.

"Hi you guys!" She was beaming. "I thought that was you. What a coincidence!"

"Well, well, young Tamsin," said Sean, "it seems we can't get rid of you no matter where we go."

"Just like a bad penny," Tamsin said with a laugh.

"Where are you headed?" Tom asked.

"I'm just following my nose. I don't have any great plans. Today, I thought I should take a look at Stonehenge."

"That's where we're going," said Tom very happily. "Let's all go together."

Many people are disappointed when they first see Stonehenge. Some because the monument seems much smaller than they had envisioned, some because its setting is not in a wild, remote location but is bordered on three sides by busy highways, and others because the site's fame has necessitated its becoming so controlled and regimented. Sean remembered his father telling him he had visited Stonehenge in the 1970s, when he had been able to park by the roadside and just wander onto the site and mooch around the stones, touching and leaning against them.

That freedom to wander was definitely a feature of the distant past. Today there was a car park for hundreds of vehicles, concrete buildings housing a shop, a restaurant and turnstiles where visitors paid about thirty dollars each and entered a tunnel under the highway. Once they emerged on the other side, visitors found that, while they could take all the pictures they like, a roped off barrier made it clear that they could not get near the stones.

Sean, Tom and Tamsin joined the long line-up, paid their money, Tom paying for Tamsin, and trooped around the monument. Despite the restrictions, Tamsin was entranced and Tom was intrigued, but Sean was clearly unhappy. He vigorously shook his head and charged ahead, softly cursing to himself.

Tom was only too glad of the opportunity to talk to Tamsin without interruption, and they soon became deep in conversation. It was not until they heard Sean's cry that they knew anything was amiss.

"No! No! No!" Sean shouted." It's not right! I know he was here. He had to be here, but I can't feel him. I need to be closer. I must get closer!"

They watched helplessly as Sean climbed over the fence and charged towards the standing stones. He rushed to the largest of the sarsens and ran his hands over it.

This incursion was soon spotted by two attendants, who hopped the fence and approached Sean.

"I had to touch them, don't you see?" Sean screamed at the men. "I had to feel them. It's what he would have done!"

Tom and Tamsin hurried round the perimeter and anxiously stood watching the melee.

"Tell them, Tom!" Sean called out. "Tell them I wasn't trying to do any damage, for Christ's sake!"

"I'm sorry, sir, but you'll have to come with us to the office," said one of the attendants as they frog-marched him back to the tunnel.

Sean sat around in the office for twenty minutes until a police car arrived and disgorged two constables. Tom and Tamsin uneasily watched through the window.

Sean again attempted to explain why he had acted as he had done, and why he should be let off, but one of the constables handed him a ticket.

"I wouldn't care if you were Brad Pitt. I don't care who you are or why you think you had to do it," said the constable in a Wiltshire country accent. "I don't know who this doctor is that you're talking about and I don't care. You've committed a criminal offence under Section One of the Criminal Damage Act of 1971, and under the Historic Buildings and Ancient Monuments Act of 1953. You'll have to appear in magistrate's court in Marlborough in the morning."

By this time it was early evening and the light was starting to change. In the car on the way to their hotel, Sean treated the incident as a joke, and although Tom was worried, he went along. Tamsin sat in the back seat looking puzzled.

"Once you've made your court appearance tomorrow, we can go to Avebury, where you can do all the feeling you want," Tom said. "There, they let you go right up the stones. You can get some good hugging in."

They reached the hotel, and while Tom was parking the car, Sean went to check in.

"I have to go," said Tamsin. "It's getting late. I won't be able to find anywhere if I leave it any longer."

"Where are you going? Why?"

"You surely don't think I can afford to stay in a place like this? I have to scour the streets for a Youth Hostel or a cheap B & B."

"You don't have to do that," said Tom very quickly, "The room probably has one of those foldaway cots. If not, I can sleep on the couch. You'd be most welcome. I couldn't let you go wandering off into the night, especially not at dinner time."

"Are you sure, Tom? It would be a godsend for me."

"Of course I'm sure."

"Well, okay. But if there's no cot, I'm taking the couch."

In the event, there was a cot, and they dumped their bags and went down to join Sean for dinner.

Tamsin didn't want an appetizer, and ordered the scampi for the main course. Tom had whitebait and homemade Lasagne, while Sean had onion rings followed by Hunter's Chicken. There was not an extensive wine list, but they settled for several bottles of Chilean Casilero del Diablo.

It was not long before the table was littered with empty plates, dishes and wine bottles.

"Tamsin's going to share my room," said Tom. "There's a foldaway cot."

"I assumed as much," said Sean cryptically as they ascended the stairs.

~

"He's a great man, isn't he? In a way. I mean he's a wonderful actor," Tamsin said when they were in the room.

"In a way, I guess. But this new role is doing something very strange to him. I admit, he worries me."

"He'll be fine with you to look after him. By the way, thanks a million for letting me stay."

"It's no problem at all, Tamsin. Look, if you like, why don't you travel with us? I'm sure we can find a similar arrangement wherever we stay."

"Are you serious?"

"Of course I'm serious."

"That would be marvelous. To be honest, I was getting a bit scared hitchhiking in a strange country, and with limited money."

"You are very welcome. And, truth to tell, I'll be glad to have someone around if Sean pulls another stunt like he did today."

"Thank you so much, Tom. I had no set plans. And now I do."

15

After a full English breakfast the next day, they drove into Marlborough for Sean's hearing before the magistrates. Upon inquiring at the hotel, they learned that a temporary court was operating out of the town hall in Marlborough as an experiment in decentralization. Otherwise, the landlord at the pub told them, they would have had to go to Salisbury, which was an hour away and would involve considerable traffic congestion.

Situated in the High Street, the town hall was an impressive Edwardian edifice built in the Dutch style, with an elaborate bow window and balcony over the front door, above which was a huge stone carving of the Royal Arms. The courtroom, on the ground floor, was a spacious room with an elaborate ceiling from which hung a number of chandeliers, and large white arches supported by columns. Apparently, in recent years, the space had mainly been used for weddings and crafts shows, but now had provisionally reverted to its historic purpose.

They learned that this morning's proceedings were being presided over by a district judge rather than a panel of magistrates, the difference being that the former was a trained lawyer with court experience while the latter were community volunteers. There were very few people in the court, the exceptions being officials and two other people who sat apart at the back of the room, presumably the accused in cases to follow Sean's .

The arresting constable was called, and in a rather bumbling manner described the circumstances involved and the charges being brought.

"Thank you, constable," said the judge, who was a suave, middle-aged man in a three piece suit. "But we will not be redundant. To charge Mr. Dorch under two Acts is egging the pudding a little too much. We shall proceed only pursuant to the Historic Buildings and Ancient Monuments Act. How do you plead?"

Sean replied that he was guilty. He was called up and sworn in. He took the oath in a loud, clear voice which rang round the room.

"I, Sean Dorch, do solemnly, sincerely, and truly declare and affirm the evidence I shall give shall be the truth, the whole truth, and nothing but the truth."

He acted as if this were a role in a film, and Tom and Tamsin thought his performance was excellent. As indeed was his testimony, which he gave with great charm and earnestness.

In a modest tone, Sean told how he had been given the role of Dr. Dee, and had allowed himself to become too immersed in the part. In a momentary loss of judgment he had acted precipitately and incorrectly, for which he was deeply sorry.

The judge was clearly affected. "Mr. Dorch, I shall not pretend that the court is unaware that you are an actor of some standing in the United States, but we cannot allow that to sway us. However, that said, the court is impressed by your sincerity and takes into account your unfamiliarity with the customs of this country. I should add that it is possible to get close to the stones at Stonehenge by special and prior arrangement outside the normal hours of visitation. You should have investigated that possibility before rampaging all over an ancient monument. I am fining you two hundred and fifty pounds."

They came out of the town hall into bright sunlight. Sean was beaming. "That was a very polite lecture from a smooth upper class guy. I liked his pinstripe suit, didn't you? He seemed to think the cops overreacted. Between us, I think he might have been a fan of my work."

"For sure, it could have been much worse," said Tom, "but for God's sake don't make a habit of it."

"I'll try," said Sean in a tone which worried Tom.

"So, let's go to Avebury and see those other stones!"

"Agreed. Let's go!"

Although the stone circle in the village of Avebury is in some ways larger and more impressive than Stonehenge because the stones are taller and wider, the site is intersected by two roads running through the centre of the monument. The whole site is surrounded by an enormous bank and ditch, with some twelve stones being on one side of the road and the remaining eight on the other side.

Sean ambled off on his own, obviously entranced by these awesome objects which were erected—nobody is certain how—by Neolithic men some five thousand years ago. He was running up to and around the stones, flapping his arms about. He was shouting something, but Tom and Tamsin could not hear what it was.

"Is he always like this?" Tamsin asked. "I mean, every day?"

"Some days are worse than others. So far, I guess you haven't seen any of the good ones."

"Is it gradually getting worse over time, Tom?"

"I would have to say it is."

"Cripes!"

"But there's nothing we can do about it except to keep a close watch on him and try to keep him out of trouble."

"If we urge him to be more cautious, would that have the reverse effect of what we want?"

"We can try to gently keep him on the straight and narrow, but he's completely unpredictable."

Just then Sean came back to where they were sitting. "Fabulous!" He was exhilarated. "Some of these must weigh over fifty tons! The theory is that they dug huge holes with sloping sides and dragged the stones to the edge and then tipped them upright with ropes and weights."

"Using that method," said Tom, "it would have taken years and years. How many men would be needed to drag fifty tons? Maybe hundreds. I wonder what Dr. Dee would have thought."

"Well, he was here. There's no doubt about that. I can feel him all over this site. I suspect he would have been as skeptical as you are, Tom, and believed that some other force was at work. Some kind of magical force."

"Wow!" Tamsin said. "This trip is turning out to be much better than I expected. It's quite exciting."

"I'm glad you think so, young Tamsin," said Sean. "Now, on to Silbury Hill!"

They headed south on the B4003 to the main A4 highway, then west to just past the village of West Kennet. Tom pulled into a layby.

"What are we doing here?" Sean demanded. "This isn't Silbury Hill."

"I know," said Tom, "but the long barrow here is famous and was built before Stonehenge or Silbury Hill. If Dr. Dee was in this area he would have been certain to come here."

"Good point. Smart thinking, Tom."

The long barrow was a vast burial mound over a hundred metres long, twenty-five meters wide and about three metres high. They learned from an information board that the barrow was built with a central passage and five chambers in which some fifty people were entombed, before the whole thing was covered with chalk. Sean was interested, but not overly enthusiastic.

"He was here, alright, but I get the feeling he was not that impressed."

"Maybe because in his time, there would have been far less to see," said Tamsin. "The site hadn't been excavated then, so he wouldn't have been able to see inside."

"That makes a lot of sense."

"Shall we move on?"

"Sure. We can see Silbury Hill just up the road."

Minutes later, they were there. They sat in the car staring across the road at one of the most extraordinary sights in the world: the largest man-made hill in Europe, which had been built in fifteen stages over several hundred years.

"What's it for?" Asked Tamsin.

"Nobody knows," said Tom.

"What's inside it?"

"Nothing."

"When did they build it?"

"About five thousand years ago."

"Holy moly!"

"Originally, it must have served some kind of mystic or quasi-religious purpose," said Sean.

He hopped out of the car and feverishly ran across the road to the fence. His eyes were shining unnaturally.

"We'd better go after him," said Tamsin.

"You know he was here, don't you?" Sean called out to them.

"I think you must be right. How could a man like him not have come here? The place sticks out like a sore thumb. It would have been a magnet to him."

"Damn these fucking fences! I want to go up to the top!"

"It's not allowed, Sean," said Tamsin nervously. "They stopped people climbing it because it caused too much erosion."

"Nonsense! What damage could one person cause?"

"For Christ's sake, Sean, don't get arrested again. Once is

enough."

"Don't worry, children," said Sean in a determined tone. "I won't involve you. Where are we staying tonight?"

"I booked us in at the Lansdowne Strand in Calne, a few miles up the road."

"Perfect! I'm coming back here after dark."

Tamsin and Tom exchanged horrified looks, but realized there was no point in arguing with Sean when he was this eager and inflamed.

Later they checked into their hotel, which they found to be charmingly old-fashioned. Tom was grateful his room had a fold-away cot, because there was no couch and sleeping in an armchair was not an appealing prospect.

They had drinks in The Snug, which was a cozy room panelled with dark, polished wood, then moved into the dining room. Tamsin and Sean had the asparagus with truffle mayonnaise to start. while Tom had the ham hock terrine. They all decided on filet of salmon for the main course, although Sean created a small scene by insisting that the plates not include samphire, something he described as a "loathsome weed".

Sean, being unusually abstemious, drank only half a pint of bitter, but the other two shared a bottle of Chablis. Towards the end of the meal, when Tom and Tamsin were trying to decide what to have for dessert, Sean rose, went to the window, drew back the drape, and peered out. It was satisfyingly dark.

He returned to the table. "Give me the keys."

"Please Sean, don't go," Tamsin pleaded.

"Is there anything I could say to get you to change your mind and not pursue this insane adventure?" Tom asked.

"No. Give them to me. All I want is to stand on the top. It's what he would do."

Tom reluctantly handed him the keys, and Sean left without further word.

He drove back to the hill and wisely did not leave the car in the car park, but slid it into a gateway to a farmer's field. He tore his pants getting over the fence but, unconcerned, proceeded to scale the massive earthen protuberance.

It was steeper and took much longer to get to the summit than he had imagined, and he arrived at the top dishevelled and breathless.

Once there, he was exultant. He stretched out his arms and slowly did a complete turn, taking in the amazing views. He could see over the Vale of Pewsey and, beyond it, the vastness of Salisbury Plain. Huge, black storm clouds rumbled overhead and a sharp wind tore at his jacket and ruffled his hair.

Slowly at first, then more heavily, the rain started to fall, but Sean did not move. Somehow, he felt as if he were going home.

Sean's absence proved the catalyst necessary to promote the relationship with Tamsin which Tom had secretly longed for. The only customers left in the bar, they were deep in conversation, leaning across the table, their faces almost touching. Tamsin's hand was on Tom's arm.

A hotel employee went behind the bar and switched the lights off. Shooting them a knowing glance, he left, whistling softly to himself.

Taking the hint, Tom and Tamsin giggled and, rather drunkenly, tottered out of the bar. They stumbled up the stairs, Tamsin's arm around Tom's neck, his around her waist.

There was little light from any source in the bedroom, but it would not have been difficult for anyone to discern that the cot was leaning against the wall, still folded, and that they jointly occupied the bed.

Jeremy Akerman

XVI

The village of West Dropsorrow was a place of some two hundred and thirty souls who inhabited cottages and shops on either side of the arms of a crossroads. One arm led from Arundel in the south, one to Fittleworth in the north, and the others to Graffham and Bepton in the west and to the town of Horsham in the east. It was called West Dropsorrow to distinguish it from East Dropsorrow, a hamlet of four houses and a farm about half a league aroint.

All roads in the vicinity were rough, stony and poorly kept, rendering them a bumpy, stumbly ride in dry weather and a sticky, slippery one when there had been heavy rains. Sometimes, such as in floods or heavy snow storms, only Farmer Sefton's big shire horse could get through.

As the traveller entered the village from Horsham he would encounter mostly humble, ill-appointed thatched dwellings with daub and wattle walls and few, very small windows, none of them boasting glass.

On the right, just before the crossroads, was a store selling local produce and flour when it was available. Occasionally, for the small number who could afford it, the vendor sold meat, mostly hogget and mutton, and far less frequently beef. Almost every household kept hens for the eggs, and cockerels for the pot.

On the left-hand side, just after the crossroads, was the local smithy, where Kit Browne, the blacksmith, affixed cart wheels, and where horses were shod and ploughs repaired.

A little way past the smithy was the only house of any size, belonging to the parson, Mr. Grahame, whose church, dedicated to Saint Giles, was located on the Bepton road.

In the centre of the village, where the roads intersected, stood the market—some said "mercat"—cross, a stone erection some three yards high on a slightly wider plinth. It was around this monument that His Grace the Bishop of Horsham had granted permission for a weekly fair to take place between the hours of dawn and dusk. About a dozen stalls would be set up, selling all manner of items and, when crops were plentiful and surplus to the needs of the growers, additional stalls would be so abundant so as to block the roads to all traffic. On such occasions, travellers would have to circumnavigate the village by way of farm tracks.

Towards the west end of the village, before the lane which led to Doctor Dee's manor house, was a low tavern, The Bull, known for its ill-kept, filthy interior and its irascible landlord, George Plunkett. It was a place not frequented by decent folk, certainly never by the nobility or gentry, and seldom by the yeomanry.

It was not difficult to establish to what class the citizens of West Dropsorrow belonged because, according to the Queen's law, a person's class determined how they could dress, where they could live, and the kinds of jobs they and their children could obtain. Her law also commanded that all should attend church services, something the habitual visitors to The Bull found difficult and for which they were publicly flogged.

Local ne'er-do-wells Ned Pascoe and Jon Nutall were quaffing ale in The Bull when Thomasina walked through the village on the way to her father's house beyond East Dropsorrow. As she strode purposefully by, villagers cast sidelong glances of suspicion and hostility, and none more so than Nuthall and Pascoe. That she was very beautiful and walked with a proud carriage only irritated them further, but it was her flaming hair which in truth most incited their hatred.

Used to such treatment and contemptuous of it, Thomasina marched on, buoyed by the happy nature of her mission.

She enjoyed the walk, as it took her through a field of ripening corn under a mighty blue sky, and she reached the house in the afternoon. Her siblings rushed out to meet her as did the dog, the donkey and the goat.

Walter, her father, hearing the commotion in the yard and ducking his head at the door, came out of the dark cottage. "Daughter! I am surprised to see 'ee today."

"I know, father, but I have to talk to you about something mighty serious."

"Don't be telling me that 'ee have lost your place up at the big house!"

"No, it is naught like that." She looked around, embarrassed. "Go, children. Your father and I have private matters to discuss."

"This sounds like a matter of heavy woe, Daughter."

"No, it is the happiest news I bring. Master Tomos Jones of Porth yn ymyl Bwlch y Sarnau has asked to wed me!"

"Soft, Daughter, 'ee be speaking in tongues."

"No, Father." Thomasina laughed gaily. "That is the Welsh language for the place of my intended's farm."

"Who is this man? I know him not."

"He is Dr. Dee's cousin from Wales, and he is as good a man as I have ever known, save for yourself."

"Are 'ee sure about yon?"

"As sure as there are stars in the sky."

"Well, I'll not stand in thy way if he can make 'ee happy. 'Tis too bad your mother could not have lived to see this day."

'Indeed. I am sure she would have approved my choice. Thank 'ee Father, for I should not want to have acted without thy blessing."

"Take it gladly. Shall I meet this fellow?"

"As soon as I can arrange it." She threw her arms around him and kissed his hairy cheek.

"Now I must get back because I have work to do around the big house."

The gradually-setting sun was fast sinking in the sky and cast long, purple shadows onto the cobbles as she returned through the village. Ned Pascoe and Jon Nuthall were still shifting ale in The Bull and were talking with landlord Plunkett as she passed.

"In broad daylight, too!" declared Pasco. "You'd think one such as she would keep herself hidden away from decent folk."

"Aye," said Plunkett. "They do say she dances naked on the downs by the full moon. If 'tis true—and I do not doubt it—'twill bring no good to any of us hereabouts."

"I heard tell that Farmer Turner's brindle cow came to term last week, and both calves were born dead," offered Nuthall.

"No!"

"Aye, each one dried and shrivelled up."

"They do say that over Long Acre way a man's sow farrowed and not one of the weans had a mouth in its snout," said Plunkett. "All died within the day for want of nourishment."

"Strange things are astir, I tell 'ee. Forces which do make nature herself stand on end," Pascoe said.

"'Twere bad enough having her out beyond East Dropsorrow and the queer doctor up at the hall," Nuthall said, "but when they came together there was bound to be mischief."

"We've not see that last of it, I'll warrant," Plunkett announced. "Bad times are a-coming, you mark my words."

XVII

Thomasina walked on through the eerie, pink light of dusk towards the manor. Up ahead, she saw a figure on the crest of the downs. It was Tomos, waiting for her return. They both broke into a run and when they met, they fell into each other's arms and gently kissed.

"From the manner of your greeting, Thomasina, I gather I am to get an answer to my proposal. Am I correct?"

"You have guessed aright, sir…Tomos…I think you be a good man and I will have 'ee though a hundred years should separate us."

"And your father? What did he say?"

"My father gives his blessing with all his heart. He was very happy for me."

"By God, that is wonderful! I shall do everything within my power to see that you never have cause to regret this decision."

"We should pay a visit to Father soon."

"Gladly. I will go to see him before I return to Porth yn ymyl Bwlch y Sarnau to make preparations for our wedding."

"We are to be wed there?"

"If you do not object. It has been my desire to be wed in the tiny church of Saint Anno, which is on my land and lies next to my own fields."

"St. Anno. I have not heard of this saint."

"He is not widely known. But you should see the church. It is the dearest little place, with a beautiful carved rood loft."

"If it is my Tomos' dearest wish, then it shall be so. I shall be happy to be wed in the church of Saint Anno."

Arm in arm, they wandered in the direction of the manor. As they approached, a movement in the bushes indicated that Talbot was spying on them again.

They strolled on to the manor grounds and separated with a kiss in the darkened orchard. Tomos headed for the front door, Thomasina for the kitchen entrance at the rear of the house.

Just as she was about to enter, Talbot sprung out from the shrubbery and seized her by the arm. She tried to scream, but he covered her mouth with his hand.

"Now, my proud beauty. I shall have that which I have long desired."

Thomasina twisted her head around and bit his hand, at which he released her go with a loud yell.

"You vixen! Why should you spurn me, a man still in possession of his youth? I have seen you with Master Tomos and it fair turns my stomach. Why should one such as he have you and not I?"

"Because I love him, and I despise you!"

Talbot stopped and stared at her, his hot ardour turning to cold hatred. "Then we shall see what profit this so-called love brings to both of you!"

He roughly pushed her aside and stormed into the house.

~

As soon as he came in, Tomos went into his cousin's workshop. There the doctor was grinding and mixing powders which he added to a liquid preparation in a ceramic bowl.

"You spend a great deal of time upon the downs these days, cousin Tomos."

"Time is my most plentiful commodity. It should not surprise you that I choose to spend much of it outdoors, especially when the weather has been so fine, and the air is clean and wholesome."

"What you say is true. There are many good prospects to be seen upon the downs."

Doctor Dee added more powder to the bowl and gently stirred it.

"Speaking of time, cousin, did it ever occur to you why, in this country, we gauge the days and months of the year in a different fashion from across the channel?"

"I have had little dealings with the continent, so it is not a subject which has commanded my attention, but I had heard it was so."

"Ignorance and prejudice. That is why. And it persists despite my best efforts."

"Your efforts?"

"Yes. The Queen sent for me to advise her on this anomalous situation. She received me at Greenwich, which as you know is one of her six palaces. She asked me what I thought of there being one calendar in Europe and a different one in her own kingdom."

"And what was your reply?"

"I said that if she would forgive my boldness, I thought it foolish that all of Christendom did not judge the passage of time in the same way."

"Indeed?"

"She called upon my Lord Burghley—he who was lately here—and told him that I had confirmed her own opinion."

"What action did she order?"

"She bade me undertake the necessary calculations in order that we might adopt the calendar promulgated in other lands. So, neglecting my own affairs, and at great expense to myself, I laboured night and day on the task.

"I was commanded to report to three men who were charged with the Queen's government in these matters: Mr. Saville, Mr. Chambers and Mr. Digges. You see, the edict regarding time was based on the belief that the Council of Nice had made no mistakes in matters of chronology. But I determined to ascertain the exact position of the earth in relation to the sun at the time of Christ's birth."

"That would make sense," said Tomos. "What did you find?"

"As I told Lord Burghley, I found that Pope Gregory was one day out in his calculations! Well, they all agreed with me, but we felt that nothing should be made of the discrepancy, so as not to put the scheme's chances at risk. Then we took it back to the Queen, but before it could be adopted she insisted on obtaining the Church's blessing. So, in due course it was placed before Archbishop Grindal and Bishops Young, Piers and Aylmer."

"That is extraordinary! What did they decide?"

"Shameful to relate, they persuaded the Queen to reject it."

"Upon what grounds?"

"You will scarcely believe this, cousin, but it was rejected because the clergy thought that, since it originated in Rome, it must be a Catholic plot! Thus was science thwarted by bigotry and prejudice."

Just then, they became aware of Talbot's presence in the workshop. He had entered so quietly, none had heard him. He now stood, hovering behind his master, a vicious look upon his face.

"Cousin, you must excuse me. Talbot and I have important work to do. We are to commune with the angels."

"May I not watch?"

"Well, I am not sure ..."

"Alas, Master," Talbot interposed quickly, "the spirits have made it clear that they would be greatly displeased by an additional presence. Indeed, they are already deeply troubled by some matter as yet unknown to me."

"Well then, Tomos, I must bid you withdraw. We must not provoke the angels."

As Tomos left the room, there was a look of great triumph on the face of Talbot. As he turned to watch Tomos go, he was jubilant indeed.

As Tomos was about to ascend the stairs to his chamber, Thomasina ran out of the kitchen and threw herself into his arms.

"Why Thomasina! What is amiss?"

"Talbot! The swine attempted to assault my person."

"No! When did this outrage occur, my love?"

"Not ten minutes since."

"I shall go and horsewhip the insolent dog this very minute!"

"Tread very carefully, Tomos. You know he has great influence over the master."

"Yes, you are arigtht. We must proceed with caution. He didn't —?"

"No! I should like to see him try! I should have clawed his eyes out."

"What a wonderful woman you are! I have truly chosen well. I will set matters in motion to hasten our wedding day. The sooner we can get you away from here the better."

"Do you swear to me that we shall indeed be wed?"

"On my mother's grave I would swear it."

By this time they were standing in front of Tomos' chamber. Thomasina pushed the door open and gently led him inside.

~

Inside the workshop it was very dark and gloomy, the only light emanating from a single, tiny, flickering candle. Talbot and the doctor were huddled around a small, round, black cloth-covered table on which stood a crystal ball.

As Dr. Dee sat transfixed, anxiously studying every line and twitch in Talbot's face, the steward moaned and, with closed eyes, placed his face next to the ball, swaying from side to side.

"Are they with us? Do you see them?" asked the doctor expectantly.

Talbot frowned and hissed for silence. The doctor instantly obeyed and shrunk back into his chair.

After further moaning and waving of his head, Talbot finally opened his eyes. "It is no use, master. They will not come. They sent only a messenger to say that they are greatly displeased."

"But what have we done to incur such displeasure? Did they inform you?"

"We have done nothing, master. The messenger says there is another presence in this household which disturbs their peace. They will not come again while that presence is here."

"Thomasina! She is new under this roof. It must be she whose presence displeases them. I shall send her back to her father at once!"

"I think not, master. It cannot be the wench who disturbs the angels. The messenger spoke of 'he'."

"My cousin! Of course. I shall ask him to return to Wales as soon as he may arrange the journey.

"I think that would be best, master."

18

It was a dark, grey, gloomy day. There was a cool, damp wind from the west, with patches of mist rising from the surrounding fields. None of the three friends was in the best of moods as they drove out of the hotel car park.

"What's the route today, coachman?" asked Sean.

"I've had a look at the map, and it looks as if we take the A 361 through Devizes and Frome, all the way to Glastonbury, with one stop," Tom said.

"What stop? I didn't authorize such a venture. We must go straight to Glastonbury Tor! It is what he would have done."

"Hold on a second, Sean. We have to go through Wells so we might as well see the cathedral. It's supposed to be one the best in Europe. You'd like to see that, wouldn't you, Tamsin?"

"Yes, the cathedral would be very nice."

"No, I don't think I can allow this."

"Sean, do you suppose Dr. Dee came this way to Glastonbury and didn't go to see the cathedral? It had been around four hundred years before he was born? How could he resist?"

"Ah," Sean muttered. "I guess so. Alright, but we cannot tarry there over long. Where are we staying tonight? Did you book some suitable hostelry?"

"Yes, we're booked into The Crown. It's bang slap in the middle of Glastonbury, only minutes away from the Abbey and King Arthur's tomb."

"Ah yes," said Sean, brightening. "Those are obligatory for us. We know he was at each of those places."

"Sounds very intriguing," said Tamsin. "And spooky."

"Drive on, my good man!" Sean commanded imperiously.

In less than an hour and a half they came into Wells and, after driving round and round for a while, finally found a parking space. The Cathedral towered above them, a magnificent monument to medieval skill and perseverance whose front façade left them speechless.

Finally, Tamsin spoke. "Look at the detail in the stone carvings. There must be hundreds of sculpted figures. It probably took years to finish."

"Amazing!" Tom said.

"Truly," said Sean. "But I don't feel that Dr. Dee tarried long here, so neither should we. Let's go, Tom!"

They set off again and, within minutes, they could see the Tor looming above the landscape. Dark, troubled clouds seemed to almost brush the stone tower on its summit.

Because they had to go into the town and walk to the Tor, they stopped off at The Crown. It was too early to check in, so they dropped off the suitcases and, changing into their walking shoes, strode out to climb the 160 metre high, conical hill which featured in Celtic mythology and was sometimes called "the Isle of Avalon". Archaeologists are unsure of its origin, some saying it was an Iron Age fort, others that it had been an older, Neolithic labyrinth.

When they were half-way up, they took a short rest and surveyed the surrounding countryside. They could see for miles, and from the lie of the land could understand how in past ages the Tor had been a refuge from flooding.

"There it is!" Sean exclaimed excitedly. "People have been coming here for centuries. Historians, archaeologists and mystics."

"What were they all looking for?" asked Tamsin.

"Answers," Sean said mysteriously.

"Is this where King Arthur of the Round Table is buried?"

"That is supposed to be back in the Abbey," said Tom. "And he wasn't a king, there was no round table, and probably is not buried there at all."

"Party pooper!" Tamsin laughed and playfully punched Tom's arm.

"How the hell do you know who he was and where he was buried?" Sean demanded indignantly.

"I read it. Apparently, he was more or less a mercenary who hired out to the Celts when they were fighting the Saxons."

"There are many mysteries of which we yet know little," said Sean. "You would do well to keep your disbelieving and defeatist opinions to yourself."

Sean's tone was so bitter and unexpected that nothing more was said for several minutes.

Eventually, Tamsin broke the silence. "Anyway I prefer him as a king with a round table."

"So do I," Sean snapped.

They continued to climb until they reached the summit. Here the wind was quite strong and a light rain started to fall. They sheltered in the lee of the tower, huddling against the stone walls.

"He was here. You know that?"

"I didn't, but I guessed."

"There is a very strong presence here. You can't deny it."

"Sean, I can't feel the guy the way you think you can, and I have to say that stone circles and castles are places where imaginations run riot. But there is something about this hill."

"I feel it too," said Tamsin.

"Good. I'm glad you are sensitive and receptive. You know, he came here looking for the Philosopher's Stone."

"What's the Philosopher's Stone, Sean?"

"It was supposed to be the thing which could turn base metals into gold."

"Wow!"

"Over there is the abbey." Sean pointed back towards the town. "That's where we're going next. Let's see if the presence is stronger there."

Half an hour later, they stood amid the ruins of the abbey. As they wandered around the walls, Sean ran his hands over the stonework or squatted down and stared at the foundations.

"This is a powerful place, Tamsin. It has many extraordinary associations. Some accounts even insist that Joseph of Arimathea came here on foot all the way from Jerusalem. He was said to be carrying the Holy Grail."

"What's that?" Tamsin asked.

"Nobody is sure. Some say it was a chalice, some say it was Jesus Christ himself."

"No way!"

"You know the hymn *Jerusalem*, by William Blake?"

"I think I've heard of it."

"This is how it starts:"

> *And did those feet in ancient time,*
> *Walk upon England's mountains green:*
> *And was the holy Lamb of God,*
> *On England's pleasant pastures seen?*

"Blake was talking about Christ coming here. To this day many in the countryside hereabouts believe it."

"They say that Joseph of Arimathea turned his staff into a thorn bush which never lost its flowers, winter or summer," Tom said.

"Is the bush still there?" asked Tamsin.

'No. Probably never was."

Sean gave Tom a severe look, then strode on until he saw a patch of grass-covered earth outlined by stones, and a sign hammered into the earth.

"It says this is the site of King Arthur's tomb." Sean sounded disappointed by this decidedly unprepossessing display of regal power.

"That's it?"

"Apparently so."

"Not much for a great king," Tamsin said.

Sean wandered on, continuing to examine the foundations of the abbey walls. When he came to a section of the abbey where the walls stood a little higher he suddenly stopped, pointed and shouted.

"There! Right there! He had somebody with him. There were two of them."

Tom and Tamsin exchanged worried glances.

"They were digging against that wall," Sean continued. "The records say they found a quantity of elixir. The elixir!"

"What was the elixir?" asked Tamsin.

"Nobody knows," Tom said.

"Whatever it was, they found it!" Sean was shaking with excitement. "They found it right there! And Dr. Dee took it with him!"

XIX

Her Majesty the Queen owned many palaces and castles, eleven in number, and moved from one to another as the whim took her, or circumstances directed. Some she inhabited, not from preference, but because they were more convenient for state business. The Palace of Whitehall was one such. Others, like the Tower of London, she seldom visited, either because they were too forbidding and uncomfortable, or like Windsor Castle, due to the fact that they were in a state of disrepair.

The distance of some from London, such as Hatfield, made them less convenient for Her Majesty. Even those at Hampton, Oatlands and Enfield involved a day's journey to reach them if weather made the roads impassable, or there was some blockage on the Thames.

It grieved the Queen that some palaces, such as Nonesuch, were built by her father, but had been sold by her sister Mary to the Earl of Arundel, and she swore that one day she would regain it for the crown.

When Her Majesty moved, the entire court moved with her, some members often getting left behind if her decision to move was precipitate. It also meant that when she shifted to one of the smaller palaces, accommodation for some could be incommodious or primitive, even though they might be earls and knights.

Her favourite home was Placentia Palace at Greenwich, where

both she and her father had been born, and which she could reach by river boat within an hour or two.

It was here that, this day, she was gathered with her Privy Council, a body comprising one fewer than twenty nobles and officials who advised Her Majesty, but could not overrule her. The council met almost every day and constituted the most influential section of her government, although it was her Secretary of State and Lord Treasurer who most often possessed her ear.

The Privy Council meeting had been proceeding for several hours, longer than was customary. Most members would rather have been at their country estates, enjoying the sight of high-flying birds, the sound of bees and the smell of new-cut hay, than sit in this dark, crowded and stuffy hall.

Hauling up his portly frame, My Lord Burghley addressed the body.

"The Queen wishes to give as a free gift the sum of 1,500 pounds to her trusty and well-beloved servant Phillip Sydney, in consideration of services wherein she has employed him and toward the payment of his debts thereby grown." Burghley looked around the chamber. "I assume there are no objections?"

The Council members knew well that Phillip Sydney was a nephew of the Queen's favourite, Robert Dudley, Earl of Leicester, and that she greatly admired his poems. There was talk that Sydney would be knighted by the Queen in the New Year. In possession of this knowledge, it would have been a foolish man who raised difficulties about this request, although privately many thought it too generous and that the recipient was not as deserving as themselves.

"Now, My Lords, give me your attention." The Queen spoke, clearly and strongly. "Tell Us this, we pray you, what do they deserve that plot against Us with foreign sovereigns?"

There were gasps and an outbreak of muttering around the table.

"It would call for the most severe punishment which can be meted out," cried Sir Christopher Hatton.

"They have deserved death," said Howard, Earl of Northhampton.

"Indeed. Death is the least of it," Sir Thomas Luvington pronounced.

"I do not doubt," said the Earl of Leicester, "that the so-called Scottish Queen is behind it."

"Would that the traitors were here. I would slay them with my own sword," spoke up Sir John Scudamore.

From his place next to Her Majesty, Sir Francis Walsingham closely observed the reactions of the Council, taking careful notes with his quill.

"Hear this!" commanded the Queen, "We have received reports of such treachery and wish to advise that any who assist it, or have knowledge of it and do not report it to Sir Francis immediately, will be shown no mercy."

While the Queen was speaking, a messenger entered and, approaching Lord Burghley, handed him a dispatch. He examined it quickly then leaned across and whispered in Her Majesty's ear.

"We are informed there has been a development in the matter," said the Queen, "so We will withdraw and take counsel with My Lord Treasurer and the Secretary of State forthwith. The Council shall meet again at Our Command."

Her majesty rose and swept out of the chamber, Burghley and Walsingam following in her wake. Shortly, they were ensconced in her private closet.

"You say this came from our trusty servant, Dr. Dee?"

"It is so. He has dated it so it is quite current, having only taken two days to reach us."

"What say you, Walsingham?" asked the Queen of Sir Francis, who had been carefully studying the missive.

"Your Majesty, Master Dee says here that his contacts in Spain have confirmed that King Phillip is planning an invasion of this country with a massive armada, although he notes it is the thinking of the King that it will take two years, maybe more, to build and assemble a fleet of the size envisioned."

"Does he say that, in this endeavour, King Phillip has conspirators in this country?"

"Indeed, he does. He specifies that the traitor or traitors are at Court."

"At Court!"

"And on the Privy Council itself!"

"God's death!" exclaimed Her Majesty. "What names does he supply? Let me have them. They shall not survive the night with their heads intact!"

"Alas, Madam, he has no names to provide. At least, not as yet. He is making further inquiries."

"I see," said the Queen. "The faithful Doctor Dee has done well. Burghley, make sure that all of the sum I promised him is forthcoming."

"Certainly, Madam. At once."

"This also means, Burghley, that we must be more circumspect at Council meetings in future and ensure that no matter comes before them which might provide information which would be to King Phillip's advantage."

"I shall see to it, Your Majesty."

20

Later that evening, after Tamsin, Tom and Sean had properly checked into The Crown, they went to their rooms to freshen up before dinner. To their pleasant surprise, Sean was in the Bruce Springsteen Room while Tom and Tamsin had been allocated the Dolly Parton Room. They found the hotel extremely comfortable and were happy to see that it had old wooden floors and furniture.

Sean was in an expansive mood when they gathered in the dining room and, believing the day to have been an unqualified success, announced that they would be celebrating with a bottle of Taittinger Brut Reserve to start off their meal. They enjoyed the Champagne while they were mulling over the menu, Sean and Tamsin choosing the pan-fried duck breasts for their main course, and Tom having the lamb chops. For their appetizer they each made different choices: grilled squid for Sean, mushroom and coconut soup for Tamsin and roast pork belly for Tom. Sean ordered a Rioja Gran Reserva to drink with the meat.

Tamsin was glad that Sean was in a happy, relaxed state throughout the meal because she had noticed an increasing tenseness in the relationship between him and Tom, and did not like where she thought it might be heading. But after they had finished eating, Sean seemed to become edgy once more.

"Have you guys known each other for a long time?" she asked.

"Oh yes," said Sean pointedly, "since before you were born."

"That's nonsense, Sean," interposed Tom.

"Well, we were at drama school together, and that wasn't yesterday."

"Do you always go on trips together? You know, to research your roles, like you are doing now?"

"No, it's the first time we've done it."

"And it may be the last," Sean said. "Tom refuses to take this seriously. This is the most challenging role I've ever had, but all Tom does is debunk my efforts to succeed. He makes a big joke out of everything. It's a good thing I met Eddie. He doesn't think it's at all funny. He takes me seriously."

"Who the hell is Eddie?"

"A local I met in the bar."

"Today?"

"Yes, before dinner."

"That was fast work."

"When people are really *simpatico*, it doesn't take long to establish friendships."

There was an uneasy silence.

"Please excuse me, I must go to the little girl's room," said Tamsin, rising.

"I'm sorry, Sean," said Tom when she had left, "I didn't know you felt that strongly about it."

"I'm trying to get into the role and you seem to be trying to stop me."

"That's crazy!"

"Is it?"

"I kid around because I think you are taking this much too seriously. You should see yourself prancing about. And you should hear yourself, too. Even your voice is changing, and you're starting to use archaic expressions."

"I can't accept that." Sean's eyes narrowed. "It's a preposterous suggestion."

"If you want, I'll try not to be so...irreverent from now on. But I wish you would calm down. It's just a role. You've had dozens before and will have dozens more in the future."

"It's not just a role!" Sean shouted across the table. "But you can't see that!"

"What on earth are you saying?"

"Nothing. Forget it. Eddie understands, even if you don't."

Another silence descended. At length, Sean said, "Changing the subject, I see that things are really going with a bang between you and Tamsin. Or should I say, lots of bangs?"

"Oh very funny! Please don't be crude, Sean. I really like this girl. To tell the truth I am falling for her."

"Well, don't fall too far." Sean frowned and lowered his voice. "You know who she is, don't you?"

"What do you mean?"

"She's in the script."

"In the script?"

"Yes. Surely, you don't think it's pure coincidence we ran into her?"

"What the hell do you mean? What on earth are you talking about when you say she's in the script?"

"Be careful, Tom. She's the witch," said Sean conspiratorially, and, leaving Tom gaping in amazement, he got up and walked away.

Tom was pouring himself some more wine when Tamsin came back from the toilets. "Where's Sean? Is everything okay?"

"He's gone, I don't know where. Probably drinking with Eddie."

"Who is this Eddie?"

"Your guess is as good as mine. Sean said he was a local. Probably, he's a regular in the bar and has been flattering Sean in order to cadge drinks from him."

"I hope he doesn't lead Sean into any more trouble. Not that he needs much leading."

"Indeed not. Incidentally, he says you're the witch."

"A witch?"

"Not a witch, *the* witch."

"What on earth do you mean?"

"Sean says you are the witch who appears in the movie script."

"What? Jesus! Is he going completely nuts?"

"I've been wondering that myself," Tom said. "Do you want another drink, or shall we go up?"

"Let's go up."

~

In the bar, an increasingly drunken Sean was holding court to about half a dozen locals. One was Eddie, a long-haired young man dressed in working clothes, suggesting he was a labourer of some kind. The others, all drinking pints of ale, ranged in age from thirty to sixty, but were of the same socio-economic demographic, speaking in the local Somerset dialect.

It was clear that each of them had seen Sean in one movie or another, and were asking him details about the productions, and especially about the female stars who had appeared with him. Most, like Eddie, were complimentary and sycophantic; but one burly fellow, George, seemed to be taking umbrage at what he believed to be Sean's condescending attitude.

"Just because you're some kind of movie star doesn't mean you can come in here and talk down to us."

"Who does not understand should either learn or be silent," Sean snarled at him.

"Now, just a minute!"

"A pox on thee!" Sean said, slurring his words.

"Watch it, mate," George countered. "You're looking for a good thumping."

"Cool it, George," urged Eddie. "He doesn't mean any harm."

"Thou art a scurvy knave!" Sean persisted with a dramatic gesture.

"Eddie, if you don't get him to stop, I'm going to give him a bunch of fives."

"Silence, fool!" shouted Sean. "Thou lard-bloated footfall!"

"Right!" George was shifting in his chair.

The barman, who had been attracted by the commotion, started to come round the bar.

"Thy vile canker-blossomed countenance curdles milk," Sean said, staggering to his feet and gripping the edge of the table. "Thy dank cavernous tooth-hole consumes all reason!"

"You've really asked for it now, you fucking Yank!"

Before George could get to him, Sean heaved the table on to its end, scattering pints and smashing glasses.

Seeing this, the barman quickly retreated back behind the bar and reached for the telephone.

Sean continued to stumble around the room, jabbing his finger at George who was being restrained by Eddie. "You whining mammet," he yelled, waving his arms in the air, "you green sickness carrion."

Several of the men grabbed Sean and pinned him to the wall, while Eddie and another man held George at bay.

"I'll fucking smash his useless American face in!"

"Thou loon!"

"Asshole!"

"Blistered be thy tongue, villain!" Sean slurred as he helplessly sank to the floor.

Summoned by the barman, the police arrived promptly. They asked who was responsible for the ruckus and the damage. The barman had no hesitation in fixing the blame squarely on Sean, and the others present murmured their agreement. Only Eddie made a half-hearted defence of Sean, saying he was a stranger who had had too much to drink.

This made no impression on the two constables, who hauled Sean to his feet and dragged him out to the police car.

Tamsin was snuggled up to Tom in bed when there was a pounding on their bedroom door. A voice came from the corrior. "Mr. Johnson! This is the assistant manager. Mr. Johnson!"

Tom and Tamsin exchanged puzzled glances as he slipped out of bed and, in only his shorts, opened the door. "What's all the fuss?"

"Mr. Johnson," said the flustered young man, "I'm afraid your friend, Mr. Dorch, has been arrested."

"Arrested?" Tom and Tamsin asked in unison.

"I'm afraid so. There was an altercation in the bar and Mr. Dorch caused some damage. He has been taken to the police station."

"Holy cow! Where is the police station? We'd better go there."

"It's in Street. That's the next town. About two miles away."

"Okay, thank you. I assume you will put the cost of any damage on the bill?"

"Oh yes, Mr. Johnson, you can be sure of that. Well, I'll say good-night, then."

~

With some difficulty, Tom and Tamsin managed to find the place, and immediately inquired about Sean.

"And who might you be?" asked a fat sergeant at the desk.

"We're friends of Mr. Dorch. We're travelling with him."

"I see. So what do you think I can do for you at this hour of the night?"

"Please, could we see Mr. Dorch?"

"I'm sorry, sir, that won't be possible. We're going to be holding him here tonight and he'll be arraigned in court in the morning. You can see him in court."

Tamsin became aware of a loud voice somewhere inside the police station. "Is that him?" she asked.

"Oh that's him, alright."

"What's he saying?"

"He's been raving on since we brought him in. A lot of nonsense, if you ask me."

They listened carefully to the hollow, eerie sound. If they had not been told by the sergeant it was Sean, they would not have recognized his voice.

"I know most assuredly," his voice intoned, "that this land never bred any man whose account therein can evidently be proved greater than mine."

21

Tom and Tamsin had a very sombre breakfast the next morning. They ate little, Tamsin having only toast and Tom settling for a single boiled egg. They were dreading Sean's court appearance, and their fears of its consequences had affected their appetites.

"They're bound to have a record of his nonsense at Stonehenge," said Tom. "So, this being his second offence, they are likely to go pretty hard on him."

"You don't think he'll be sent to prison?"

"I doubt it, but it's possible. If it's a fine, I think it will be heavy, maybe as much as five hundred pounds."

"Holy moly! That much? That's like $800, isn't it?"

"Something like that. I'm just guessing about the fine. But don't worry on that score, Tamsin, he's got the money."

"Okay. But you know what does worry me, Tom?"

"What?"

"I'm afraid that he'll misbehave in court. Go into one of his weird performances, and start flapping his arms about."

"If he does, they will either throw the book at him, or send him to a psychiatric facility."

"That would be terrible," Tamsin said. "If that did happen, what would happen to you and me?"

"I've been thinking about that, sweetheart. If he gets any worse, I wonder if we should split from him, hire our own car, and go off on our own."

"I'd like that. And he is getting worse. I wonder if this Eddie had anything to do with last night."

"It wouldn't surprise me. I have a bad feeling that we haven't heard the last of Eddie."

The courtroom was quite small and, apart from officials and one old lady sitting at the back, the seats were empty when Tamsin and Tom filed in. The bench was occupied by three magistrates and an advising lawyer.

The magistrates on either side were grey, seemingly mild-mannered, middle aged men, likely shopkeepers or tradesmen. However, the one in the middle looked like a battleaxe from an old English movie.

The clerk announced that the Honourable Mrs. Letitia Redfern-Digby would be presiding. She was elderly, but as upright as a ramrod, snotty and nanny-like, with rimless spectacles perched on the end of her nose, and purple tints in her white hair. When she spoke, her voice was very loud and 'cut glass'.

"Bring up the accused!" she barked.

Sean emerged from below floor level, where they had been holding him in the temporary cells. Looking hung-over and extremely sheepish, he mounted the stairs and appeared in a raised, pulpit-like box.

The clerk read the charges, to which Sean pleaded guilty. A statement was given by the arresting officer, whereupon the magistrates consulted, whispering to each other. Their nodding heads indicated that they were agreed on a sentence, and that the two on either side had given the battleaxe free rein to deal with the miscreant.

"Mr. Dorch," she began in a severe, disdainful tone, "your behaviour has been utterly outrageous and unforgivable. Without any apparent gesture towards propriety and good manners, you proceeded to get disgustingly intoxicated, started a loud argument in a public place, grossly and obscenely insulted other people, and caused not inconsiderable damage to private property. There is some question as to whether or not you resisted arrest, so we will set that aside."

She glowered at him while she took off her glasses and polished them with a Kleenex. Then she held them up to the light to examine the lenses.

"Thank you, your honour," said Sean.

"Be quiet! I haven't finished. And I am not 'your honour', I am 'Your Worship'," she snapped, replacing the glasses on her nose. Even the other two magistrates seemed afraid of her and they slightly edged away from her as she raised her voice to a new pitch.

"This is an exceedingly serious matter and I don't mind telling you I am not in the least inclined to show the slightest leniency. Particularly not in light of information provided by the police to the effect that some days ago you appeared before my learned colleague for trespassing and attempting to deface an ancient monument. Disgraceful!

"I know your type, indeed I do. You Americans think that, because you have money or are so-called celebrities, you can do what you want and behave like savages. Well, not on my patch, you can't!

"By rights I should give you a custodial sentence, but I see no reason why the British taxpayer should house and feed you. I fine you a thousand pounds—I wish it could be more—plus court costs, and I order you to make recompense to the Crown Hotel for damages incurred.

"Finally, I warn you in the strongest possible terms that you had better be on your best behaviour for the remainder of your visit here. That is all. You may go."

The magistrates rose and filed out of the court. The policeman conducted Sean over to the clerk who, in turn, referred him to the official who collected the fines. The procedure took some time as there were forms to fill out and a check had to be made on Sean's credit card.

When they were in the car, Sean was subdued.

"Cheer up," said Tom, "you're not the first movie star to have a criminal record."

Sean just grunted.

"According to the itinerary, our next place of interest is Westbury-on-Severn, where Dr. Dee had a rectory."

"Good," muttered Sean. "Have you fixed somewhere to say tonight?"

"Yes. You will like this, I promise. We are staying at a four-hundred-year-old Tudor hotel called The Feathers, in Ledbury. The food is supposed to be spectacular and it is only about half an hour's drive from Westbury."

"That sounds wonderful," Tamsin said. "Is it one of those black and white places?"

"Yes. I think they call it 'half timbered'."

"Oh, good!"

"Four hundred years old?" Sean asked.

"Yes. It may be even older."

"That means Dr. Dee could have been there?"

"Exactly. I thought you'd like that. Well, we'd better go and check out, and you have to square the owners for the table and glasses."

"Alright," said Sean, passing Tom a piece of paper. "Then we have to go to this address."

"What is it? Why do you want to go there?"

"It's where Eddie lives."

"Eddie?"

"Yes. He's coming with us."

22

Checking out of The Crown took longer, and was more complicated, than they expected. The manager could not compute the total cost of damage caused by Sean until one of the company's assessors could come from Yeovil, some eighteen miles away.

They cooled their heels in the lounge until the Assessor finally arrived, studied the situation and presented Sean with the bill, which he paid with his credit card. The manager was quite polite, even friendly, about the matter, saying that, apart from the incident in the bar, it had been a pleasure to host such a distinguished guest.

Before leaving, Tom asked the manager for directions to the address Eddie had given to Sean, but even so he managed to get lost, and it was at least half an hour before they arrived at a narrow, run-down house, one in a row of ten in a back street.

Eddie, who had been waiting at the front door, bounded out into the street. He was an angular, ungainly young man in his mid-twenties, wearing a tee-shirt, jeans, a cheap anorak and worn-down dress shoes. He had long, dark hair down to his collar, and large, inflamed, red acne on his face. Over his shoulder he had slung a backpack, clearly containing only the bare necessities.

"Good afternoon Eddie," Sean called out.

"I bin looken out var'ee," Eddie replied, "How be on?"

"Fine, Eddie."

"Whirr zer bin to?"

"I had to appear in court, but apart from that, I'm in one piece."

Tom and Tamsin exchanged puzzled glances. They were amazed that Sean seemed to understand the Somerset dialect which, to them, seemed like a foreign language.

"How be on, zir," Eddie said to Tom, and to Tamsin said, "Alright, me luvver?"

Eddie climbed in the back with Sean, shook his proffered hand rather limply, and proceeded to scratch himself in the groin. "That George were a spuddling last night," he said to Sean. "But you were a beskummering him sumthen wicked. Too much Zumerset zyder, cordin eye."

"You're right there, Eddie. I had a real skinful."

"Arr. So, whirr agoan?"

"North to Ledbury. Do you know it?"

"Eye niver bin, but Eye had a ninny-watch to see them parts. What'll eye do fer a chimmer? Eyem skint."

"You can share my room. Don't worry about money, Eddie. We'll stay in Ledbury, then we're going to Upton tomorrow. It's where Dr. Dee once lived."

"Tha'll be gert."

"Are we ready for the off?" asked Tom.

"Yes, let's go. What's the itinerary?"

"It's ninety miles, so it should take us about two hours. We'll take the A39 to Bridgewater, then the M5 north, then the M50 west and finally the A417 to Ledbury."

"I reckon yon swallowed the map," said Eddie with a snicker.

"I hear there are many strange tales about these parts," said Sean. "I think you believe them, don't you?"

"Oh, arr, Eye believes it alright."

"Tell us about the weirdest ones."

"There's the road tween Nunny and Frome fer starters. All manner of folk sees strange visions there."

"What do they see?" Tamsin asked.

"Folks appearin on the road. Itchikers, they do say. The dead thumbin fer a ride in the dimpsey."

"What's dimpsey?"

"Day's end when sright nottlin, and dark an grey."

"I'm sorry, Eddie," said Tamsin, "but I have difficulty understanding you."

"That's because you're out of synchronicity," Sean said.

"Synchronicity?"

"Yes, incidents of significance ask us to dampen our self-obsession and consider the possibility of the strange or unknown."

"I don't know what you mean."

"You don't seem to understand that the dialect Eddie speaks is much closer to early modern English than the way we talk," said Sean, "that means that Dr. Dee would likely have spoken like Eddie. That's why Eddie is so important to me: he brings me closer to the doctor."

"I guess we'll learn to understand you in time, Eddie," said Tom.

"Ifn you does, twill be a proper job." Eddie laughed.

"Tell us some other stories," urged Sean.

"There's Molly at Yeovil station, fer one."

"Who is Molly? Please explain."

"Hers a tea lady what died sixty year since, yet folk sees er on the platform at the station."

"Creepy!"

"Then there's ghosts in the old asylum at Barrow Gurney. I ant seen em, but plenty ave."

"A derelict mental asylum is a natural for strange events," said Sean. "What else?"

"You can't go wrong with Wookey 'Ole. Caves and that. Manys the one bin auverlooked by them caves."

"Auverlooked?"

"It means bewitched," said Sean.

"There were ghosts in the prison," Eddie said solemnly.

"You were in prison, Eddie?" Tamsin was surprised.

"Ar fer a bit. In the Mallet, I was."

"He means Shepton Mallet," Sean explained. "It's a town about half an hour from here."

"I just love the names of the places around here. Can you give me some more, please Eddie?"

"Lemme see. There's Nepnett Thrubwell."

They all laughed.

"I got better," said Eddie. "Velvet Bottom."

More laughter.

"That's a good one," said Tom.

"Then there's Puddin' Pie Lane in Langford, and Butt's Batch in Wrington."

"The names are magical," said Tamsin.

"Exactly!" Sean affirmed.

"Tinker's Bubble."

"That's lovely."

"Sticklepath, and Nimmer. That's all I can think on right now."

~

They arrived in Ledbury in the late afternoon. On the drive, Sean had been looking up the town's history on his phone, and now informed the others of its prominent features.

"The town dates from the seventh century, so it featured in Saxon, Norman and Elizabethan history as well as the civil war. It was a stronghold of the cavaliers and saw four battles."

"Four!" cried Eddie. "Proper job!"

"Elizabeth Browning was born here."

"How do I love thee, Let me count the ways," Tamsin said.

> *I love thee to the depth and breadth and height.*
> *My soul can reach, when feeling out of sight.*
> *For the ends of Being and Ideal Grace.....*

"We learned this in school," said Sean, chiming in dramatically:

> *I love thee to the level of every day's,*
> *Most quiet need, by sun and candlelight.*
> *I love thee freely, as men strive for Right;*
> *I love thee purely, as they turn from Praise;*
> *I love thee with the passion put to use.*
> *In my old griefs, and with my childhood's faith.*
> *I love thee with a love I seemed to lose*
> *With my lost saints, love thee with the breath,*
> *Smiles, tears, of all my life!—and, if God choose,*
> *I shall but love thee better after death.*

"That's so sad," said Tamsin.

"If you ask me, it's a bunch of northering vlother," said Eddie. "You says you don't unnerstand me. I couldn't unnerstand a word of that there!"

Everyone joined in his laughter.

"And Elizabeth Hurley was born here..."

"Oo, nice bit o' crumpet, her," said Eddie.

"And Robertson's Golden Shred marmalade used to be made here."

"Maybe we'll get some with our breakfast," said Tom, as he eased the car through an archway into the hotel parking lot. "Here we are."

They all adored The Feathers, except Eddie, who was over-whelmed by its luxury and felt out of place. Its antiquity, sumptu-ous rooms and furnishings were just what the others had been hoping for.

~

As they settled into their beautiful room, Tamsin touched Tom on the arm. "Er…is Sean…gay?"

"Sean? Good God, no. He might be bi for all I know, but I've never heard about it. Why do you ask?"

"It seems strange, Eddie sharing his room."

"Eddie couldn't afford a room, and Sean probably wants to limit the expense. A place like this isn't cheap."

"I guess you're right. What do you make of him?"

"Who, Eddie? He's a strange duck and no mistake. But not offensive. At least, not so far."

"I think it's hilarious the way he talks. I'm just about getting one word in five."

"I think I'm getting one in seven."

~

They gathered in the charming, comfortable bar for drinks, where Tamsin had a white wine and Tom a Balvenie single malt Scotch. Eddie, embarrassed, asked for a pint of ale, and Sean, to make him feel less self-conscious, ordered the same. Later, they moved into the large, beautiful dining room for dinner.

To start, Tamsin ordered mussels, Tom the rabbit pappardelle, and Sean the soup.

Eddie seemed confused. "I'm fer fish and chips," he said in whisper. "If I has soup along with you, does it mean I canst have the fish and chips?"

"No, you can have both." Sean chuckled. "Have whatever you want!"

"That's proper job! That's my verdit."

For their main courses, Sean had the slow roasted pork belly and Tamsin the vegetable curry, while Tom went for the ribeye steak. To drink, Sean ordered a bottle each of Sancerre and Barolo.

"This is some chaity nosset," said Eddie.

"It is very good food," Tamsin agreed.

"Shall we feel the doctor tomorrow, I wonder?" asked Sean.

"If 'ees there, I'll know it," Eddie said with conviction.

XXIII

Doctor Dee sat at his writing desk in no inconsiderable degree of discomfort and indecision. Talbot had told him what he must do, but he was greatly loath to be inhospitable to his cousin. Could Talbot be wrong? He had known many men who were great scholars who had still made mistakes, so why not this man, he who had little learning and no manners? Moreover, the doctor was finding Talbot, who was now standing behind him wringing his hands, to be increasingly annoying in his oleaginous and fawning ways.

"I admit that it has been weeks since the angels came to visit us. I need their guidance. What am I to do?"

"I have told thee, Master. You know what must be done," said Talbot in his oily, minatory fashion. "His presence offends them and they will not come again while he is under your roof. I know not why this should be so, but while he is here, they will stay at some remove."

"Could you not be mistaken, Talbot? Surely there could be some other reason for their absence. Might it not be that their presence had been urgently required elsewhere?"

"It may be, Master, but the only way you could discover the truth of the matter would be to send Master Jones away and see what happens. Then if the angels continue to desert us, you could bring him back after a time."

"There is indeed some logic in what you say. Very well, it shall be done. I am reluctant to treat a kinsman so badly, especially when he is here at my invitation—nay, as a result of my entreaties. But I see there may be no other way."

"None that suggests itself, Master."

"Alright. Be so good as to ask my cousin to meet me in the garden at noon."

"At once, Master."

At the appointed hour, the doctor went forth into the garden, where he found Tomos waiting upon him. Dr. Dee was sorely troubled and much uncomfortable with the task at hand.

"Walk with me, cousin, I beseech you."

"Certainly. It would be my pleasure. Where shall we walk?"

"Upon the downs. Let us go as far as the grove of lime trees."

The two men sauntered onward in silence, the doctor holding his head down as he walked. Tomos surmised that something was amiss, but he said nothing, and thought it best to wait until the doctor spake again.

"You will remember what I told you about the spirits—I call them angels—coming to assist me in interpreting the natural phenomena around us?"

"I do."

"They have not been coming for some weeks now."

"That is most unfortunate. Are you sensible of the reason?"

"It saddens my heart to have to say this, cousin, but it would seem that you are the reason."

"Me!?"

"Yes, the angels stay away because, for some reason unknown to me, they object to your presence in the house."

"May I ask how you came to know this?"

"Talbot tells me it is so."

"Ah!" Tomos' lip curled. "I should have guessed!"

"I understand you have antipathy for the man, but I have no other choice if I am to continue my work and studies. I hope you will not think me too unkind if I beg you to leave?"

"Not unkind. Perhaps misguided. As you say, you know how I feel about that ill fellow."

"Well, then, maybe it is for the best that you be parted from him."

"From him, yes, but not from Thomasina."

"Thomasina? How does she signify in this?"

"I will tell you plainly, cousin, that I have formed a powerful attachment to the girl, and she has consented to be my wife."

"Your wife! How comes it that I have no inkling of this news? This arrives as a complete surprise to me."

"I have kept it to myself this long because I waited until she was sure it was her desire also."

"That, I can understand in the circumstances. Have you addressed yourself to her father?"

"I have, and he is agreeable."

"Then, cousin, I would say you are fortunate. Marriage is an honourable estate I would recommend to any man who can afford to sustain it. As you know, Jane is my second wife."

"Indeed. And I do count myself exceeding fortunate. Would that I could take her with me now, but it would be unseemly. As soon as I have made arrangements for the wedding at Llananno and at Porth yn ymyl Bwlch yn Sarnau, I shall return with a carriage and a maidservant to accompany her to Llanbister, where she shall reside at The Lion until we are wed at St. Anno's church in Llananno."

"Ah, Saint Anno's! You have chosen well. I love that little church with its beautiful rood screen. Though it be dedicated to a Catholic saint, you could not have picked a better place. But you had best not issue too many invitations, or you not get the people into the church."

"I would crave a special boon, cousin."

"Name it."

"I pray you will keep a close eye on my bride while I am gone. I tell you plainly, I do not trust Talbot's designs upon her. I will not dwell on it, but I have reason to believe he has already made advancements towards her."

"I am sorry to hear this." Dr. Dee frowned deeply. "You have my word that I shall speak to him and forbid any such endeavours in the future. It is the least I can do to make amends for my breach of hospitality."

"I thank you, most kindly. Now I go to see her father Walter and advise him of my plans."

"That is meet. May God go with you."

~

Within the hour, Tomos was at Walter's house, where Thomasina was drawing water from the well. She ran to him and they embraced warmly.

"I see your horse is loaded and packed," she said, a tear in her eye, "So you are going to Wales. How long will you be gone, my love?"

"I reckon it will take me five days each way, and a few days at the farm. Maelgwyn is a very strong horse. Born and bred on my own farm. Though he be an ambling nag, he is, as you can see, nearly sixteen hands. I should be back inside two weeks."

"Two of the longest weeks of my life," Thomasina sobbed. "Here comes father."

"Good morrow, Walter!"

"Good morrow, Master Tomos. I see you are arroint."

"I am indeed."

Tomos repeated to Walter what he had told the doctor, and all his proposed arrangements met with the man's approval. They shook hands warmly, whereat the father retreated inside the dwelling so Tomos and Thomasina might say their last goodbyes.

"As soon as I get to Wales, I shall see the parson and arrange our wedding. When all is in readiness, I shall return to take you back to be mistress of Porth yn yml Bwch y Sarnau."

They embraced and kissed passionately.

Finally, Tomos swung into his high saddle, and clucked to Malelgwyn to commence his long journey. His pack and bags jingled as the huge, black animal moved forward.

Through his study window, Dr. Dee had watched Tomos ride off in the direction of Walter's house. He was troubled and sad as Talbot joined him at the window.

"It is for the best, Master. Your work is too important to be sacrificed for lesser considerations," said Talbot obsequiously.

Dr. Dee seemed uncertain and did not reply, casting his eyes away from the window to his desk.

"Do not be downcast, Master. The mails are here. Perchance there is good news from Spain."

"Let us hope so. Before I open the dispatches, I need a word with you which you would do well to take to heart."

"What is that, Master?" Talbot asked hesitantly.

"Hear this: I will not have you interfere with Thomasina in any way whatever! Do you understand?"

"What is she to you? She is not kin to you," Talbot blurted hotly. "Why should I not pursue her as well as the next man?"

"Know your place!" the doctor said angrily. "How dare you speak to me in that fashion? She is betrothed to my cousin, and I will not have her touched. I forbid you to approach or harass her. I forbid it! Do you understand?"

"Yes, Master," said a greatly abashed Talbot. "I will do as 'ee asks."

"Good. Now give me those dispatches and we shall see what news there is."

Dr. Dee opened the dispatches and read the message contained therein. He read carefully for several minutes, re-read the contents, and then exclaimed triumphantly, "We have the traitor, methinks! Her Majesty will be mightily pleased. You spoke aright, Talbot. The news is very good."

The doctor sharpened his quill, pulled some vellum towards him, and hastily wrote a letter to Walsingham, the Queen's spy master. Then he dropped melting wax on to the joint and affixed his seal.

"Look lively, Talbot! See this is sent to London without delay. Make haste!"

Talbot took the dispatch and hurried off. Dr. Dee pounded his fist upon the desk. "Yes! We have the dog!"

He gazed at the seal, which was a pentagram within a hexagon, within a septagram, contained within a further septagram, and all enclosed within a circle. Indeed, he thought, it was right that the seal was known as *Sigillum Dei*, "the seal of God."

XXIV

When Talbot left his master's abode with the dispatch to London, he was in low and mean spirits. Although he granted that he himself had spoken out of turn, he greatly resented the way the doctor had given him the rough edge of his tongue and had admonished him in such strong terms. He chafed under the burden of this, and cursed the moon and stars for his lot.

If he were to remain in Dr. Dee's service, from which he derived considerable benefit, he knew he could never go against his master's direct and particular instructions. To do so would mean dismissal, and Talbot could not afford that because he knew not what he might do for his daily bread out in the world.

Suddenly, a sinister idea came into his mind, and the more he thought on it, the more determined he became. "So," said he to himself, "If I cannot have Thomasina, then so be it. But if I cannot have her, neither Jones nor any other shall have her. By God, I swear it!"

With this resolve in his mind, he approached the carter, who would take the dispatch to Horsham, and deliver it there to the special messenger Dr. Dee usually employed to carry such missives to London. He paid the carter his fee for the service and asked where he should put the dispatch.

"Put un in back, Master Talbot, but be sure 'ee makes it fast, so it don't tumble about," the carter said.

"Don't be giving me orders!" Talbot snapped. "I have plenty of those from my employer. I don't need any from the likes of 'ee!"

He went around to the rear of the wagon, and in a fit of pique hurled the package in amongst the sacks and barrels. He stalked away towards the big house, still in a foul mood, but a plan had formed in his head. He knew what he had to do to get even with the upstart Jones and with the doctor.

The carter cracked his whip and the wagon set off out of the village, bound for Horsham. The weather was fine for the first hour and, although, the road to Graffham was rough, it was nothing the big horses could not deal with.

However, at Heath End the clouds opened and it began to rain heavily, and by the time they reached Coulterhsaw Bridge, the surface had turned to mud and the great ruts became slippery and treacherous. Here, they had to cross over two bridges because the River Rother divided into two branches before rejoining each other beyond where the river flowed on to join the River Arun, hard by St. Botolphs Church.

The first of these bridges was somewhat precarious, but the carter quietened down the horses and bade them take it very slowly. But the second was not only rickety, but also slimy where the heavy rain had washed earth from a farmer's field onto the bridge. The horses slipped and slid, bucking this way and that, and the wagon slewed mightily until one wheel was hanging over the edge.

The carter, who had been at his trade for many years, knew that indecision in such a circumstance was not a recourse which would prove successful. He reckoned that the only choice before him was to whip the horses so they might spring forward and clear the bridge. This he did, and with one great scramble they were off the bridge and once more upon the highway.

But in the effort, the wagon lurched and, almost capsizing, spilled some of its contents into the foaming waters of the Rother. Among these items were a sack of flour, a barrel of pickled trotters, a wooden cage containing a ferret, and the leather pouch holding the letter from Dr. Dee to Sir Francis Walsingham.

25

The next morning they were up early and were hungry for breakfast. The hotel had a wide selection of items, all extremely appetizing. Tamsin chose a spinach, mushroom and tomato muffin with poached eggs and Sean picked the eggs Benedict, while Tom and Eddie had the full English breakfast: a huge plate containing eggs, bacon, sausage, black pudding, baked beans, hash browns, mushrooms and tomato, all of which glistened welcomingly.

Eddie ate as if he had been on a forced diet for a month and was wiping his plate with toast before the others were halfway through their meals. He was slurping tea while the others drank coffee.

"That's proper job and no mistake," said Eddie. "That's my verdict."

"So, we're off to Upton today?" Tom inquired.

"Yes, indeed," Sean affirmed. "Dr. Dee was the clergyman here for almost thirty years."

"Maybe," Tom said.

"What do you mean, maybe?" demanded Sean.

"He held the living, but that doesn't mean he lived here, or necessarily ever came here."

"I don't believe it!"

"How could that be?" asked Tamsin.

"Many ministers were given the living—that is, the income—from a church as a favour from some nobleman or landlord—or even the Queen herself. Then they would hire a curate, usually a poor lesser clergyman, to perform all the services, pay him a pittance and then live wherever they wanted on the profit."

"That ain't fair," said Eddie. "Some vinnny, if you asks me. If they tried to pull that un today, they'd be right beskummered."

"But Dr. Dee wouldn't do that," Sean insisted.

"He might have," said Tom. "I've been looking this up on Google and it seems he also held the living of St. Swithin's at Leadenham in Lincolnshire from 1566 until he died in 1608."

"He weren't no lurdin, were 'ee?" Eddie chortled.

"Sean, the point is that during that same period we know he was in Sussex. How can he have been at three places at the same time?"

"Maybe he went from one place to another," Sean said, not very convincingly.

"They are miles apart," Tom said. "It's something like a hundred and twenty miles from Upton to Leadenham and over a hundred and fifty miles from Upton to the Sussex Downs. In those days, it would have taken the best part of a week to get from one place to another."

"He has a point," said Tamsin.

"I don't know." Sean seemed lost.

"And if he had a curate at Leadenham, why not at Upton, too? It is possible—no, likely—that he never went to either place."

"Well, us'll find out today in luglain," Eddie said.

"Eddie, I have no idea what you just said," said Tamsin with a laugh. "In fact, I haven't understood half of what you've said this morning."

"There's no need for you to be betwalted about that, me luvver," said Eddie, grinning from ear to ear. "Pretty soon I'll be learning to speak right chaity like you."

"What Eddie means," Sean interrupted, "is that when we are in Upton we will know one way or another if Dr. Dee was there."

"Arr, will that." Eddie was in no doubt.

"Where do we go when we leave here?" Tamsin asked.

"Well, he was in Manchester," Sean said, "but I'm not sure what success we would have in a large city."

"I think you're right, Sean. It would be like looking for a needle in a haystack."

"Needle in a haystack!" Eddie laughed loudly. "That's proper job!"

"We haven't been to Wales, Sean," Tom said. "I know it was his early years he spent there, but Nant-y-Groes in Radnor shire is where he is from."

"Yes, that is a must, now I think about it. Is it far from here?"

"No, only about sixty miles. We could drive there in two hours."

"Then it's settled. Tom, find us some place to stay when we get there."

Less than an hour later found them wandering around the pretty little town of Upton-upon-Severn, located on a bend in a river which rises in the mountains of north Wales, sweeps around into England, and then disgorges into the Bristol Channel in south Wales.

They were enchanted by the ancient streets, the many black-and-white, half-timbered Tudor shops and houses, the quaint pubs and the walks along the riverside. Tom stepped into a small shop to buy a guide pamphlet while the others meandered through the town.

He caught up with them by the Church of Saint Peter and St. Paul, and quickly thumbed through the leaflet. "This is not the church," he announced.

"What do you mean?" Sean sounded annoyed. "We can see it in front of us, with our own eyes!"

"No, this one wasn't built until the nineteenth century. The church that was here in Dr. Dee's time was attached to that tower there." He pointed up the road to an imposing structure adorned with a strange cupola which looked like a pepper pot.

"Attached?"

"Yes. It's no longer there. Just the lower portion of the tower was here when he was. That is, if he was here."

"Don't start that again. Let's go to the other tower and see if there is a rectory nearby."

When they got to the tower, there were a number of buildings close by which might have been a rectory, but nothing which was identified as such.

"There's nothing in the pamphlet about a rectory," Tom said. "Of course, there didn't have to be one if the incumbent priest was not resident in the community. His curate probably couldn't afford a house."

"Damn!" Sean exploded. "Let's keep looking. Maybe we should knock on some doors and ask people."

"This is a gert waste of time," said Eddie suddenly. "I doan want to spuddle with you, but the trail have gone nottlin."

"Nottling?"

"Cold as the grave."

"Alright, let's go back to Ledbury."

"Can't we stay here a little longer?" asked Tamsin. "It's a lovely place."

"Yes, it is very nice," Tom agreed.

Sean reluctantly concurred and, as they walked, took the opportunity to again expound on what a great man Dr. Doctor Dee had been.

"When he went to the University at Louvain in Belgium, he was the toast of the town. Apparently, he was an inseparable companion of Gerard Mercator."

"Is that the geographer?" Tamsin asked.

"That's the one. And when he went to Paris, he gave the first free public lecture on Euclid's elements ever delivered anywhere in the world. The room couldn't hold all the people who wanted to hear him."

"Wow!" Tamsin exclaimed.

"I doan unnerstan it," said Eddie. "Sounds northerin to me."

"Where else did he travel to, Sean?"

"He went to Poland, of course, and to the College of Reims, where they wanted him to be regius professor of mathematics at two hundred crowns a year."

"That wasn't chicken feed in those days."

"It was the same at Oxford. He was offered a huge sum to lecture on mathematics, but he turned them down. too."

"His priorities lay elsewhere, no doubt," said Tom maliciously.

"Indeed," Sean said, giving Tom an icy stare. "In the 1560s he went to Hungary. He was invited by the emperor Maximillian II. Dee gave him a copy of his *Monas Hieroglyphia*, his great work on the mysteries of codes and cyphers."

"How do you know all this stuff?" Tamsin asked.

"Research. I take my roles seriously. I wish others did, too."

"Ouch," said Tom.

"Even when he was an old man, they made him head of the university in Manchester."

"Impressive," Tamsin said.

"A towering figure," Sean said pompously.

After winding up and down the streets of Upton for several hours, they returned to the car and drove back to Ledbury to the Malvern Hills, stopping at the British camp, where they parked and clambered up the iron-age hill fort. There they looked out over a vast expanse of countryside basking in the sunlight.

About sixty miles away to the west, they could see Pen y Fan, the highest mountain in central Wales. Some forty miles to the north of that peak was their destination on the following day.

"A disappointing day," said Sean when they were on the move again.

"No, it was lovely!" Tamsin said.

"I couldn't feel Dr. Dee at all. Could you, Eddie?"

"Gert waste of time. Alright for grockles, if you likes that sort of thing."

"Grockles are tourists. That means you," Sean said with satisfaction.

"You shouldn't be discouraged, Sean. I did warn you that it was likely he didn't spend time there. Probably he just collected the tithes."

"You think that, do you?" Sean flared. "Or maybe the reason is that your fucking negativism, your constantly mocking presence, is what is driving him away!"

"Jesus, just listen to yourself, Sean. 'Driving him away.' This loony tunes character is getting you all fucked up."

"You've been against him for the very beginning, haven't you?"

"What do you mean 'against him'? The guy has been dead for four hundred years, Sean! You talk about him as if he was your uncle who died last week."

"All I ask for is some respect."

"Who for? You or him?"

"Both of us deserve it."

"I've always had a lot of respect for you, Sean, you know that. But I didn't know Dee. He wasn't a saint…or God."

"He was one of the greatest minds of his age."

"I'm not disputing that. I know you admire him and I know you want to get under his skin so you can do the part better, but, for God's sake, let's keep a sense of proportion."

"I don't know what you mean."

"Don't let this dead guy fuck you up. And take a look at the other side of him, too!"

"What other side?"

"Well, for example, if he was so smart, how come he got sucked into all this crystal ball crap? How come he got totally suckered by this Talbot—who, incidentally, was using a false name, and who later admitted he was a spy planted to try to trap Dee into incriminating himself about having dealings with the devil?"

"Nobody's perfect."

"It would seem to me that one of the greatest minds of his age would have been a little more sensible when encountering con-artists and crooks."

"Now, now boys," Tamsin intervened. "Let's put a stop to this before it gets out of hand."

"Aye, we had enough of this beskummering," said Eddie glumly. "'Tis all vlother any road. Cordineye stimey wenoam!"

There was a second's silence, then they all burst out laughing.

XXVI

As Tomos departed through Bepton on his way to the small villages of Rogate, Liss and Alton, Maelgwn developed a slow, steady, almost hypnotic, rocking gait from side to side. This suited Tomos, as he always thought it better for a long journey than a trotting horse, not only for the comfort, but because the animal would become less tired. He was lucky Maelgwn was a big, healthy, strong horse, because he would be asked to walk over thirty miles a day, with only six to eight hours to rest. The journey down had been hard, but Maelgwn had been equal to the task and, for some weeks recently, had been enjoying rest and excellent feed and grazing at Dr. Dee's establishment.

The journey to the south had been relatively uneventful, but it had taught Tomos to ever be on the lookout for rogues and villains. Twice he was the victim of an attempted robbery of his person, and on another occasion a low fellow had tried to make off with Maelgwn in the middle of the night. For this reason, this time he was fully equipped with the weapons he might need on the journey. In addition to his dagger, broadsword and Welsh yew bow, he now also carried a billhook and a wheelock firearm. This latter was un-wieldy and was difficult and slow to load, so would be of little use in an immediate encounter, but might be well effective if he were pinned down by some assailants behind some rocks or trees.

He was bound for Basingstoke on the first day of his excursion. This was an ancient town which had been occupied for centuries afore the Romans came to these islands. However, Tomos knew he could not take a direct route because, from experience and hearsay knowledge, he had to avoid the Royal Forests, of which there were more than a few on his route. Not only were these places where it might be easier for footpads to lie in wait for the traveller, but also due to the fact that the Queen's forest serjeants and surveyors could be over-zealous in arresting and falsely charging innocent people.

The first of these beautiful but dangerous forests was at Woolmer, but twelve miles off. On other days there would be Buckholt, Braydon, and Feckenham to contend with and, depending upon which route he chose, also the Forest of Dean. In each case, Tomos would do his best to skirt around these royal preserves and, where possible, to stay in sight of human habitation. Since public order was highly prized in the land, and most communities, however small, were policed by The Watch, comprising armed citizens under control of the sheriff, this would render him safe much of the time.

He knew the most common crimes, theft, cut-purses, and begging, attracted severe punishments, and that the fear of these penalties had the effect of reducing offences. At least, so he devoutly hoped.

It was after dark when he rode into Basingstoke and stabled his horse at the White Hart Inn. After feeding Maelgwen and brushing him down, he went into the inn to break his fast and secure a bed. He was too late for the roasted meat, which had been capons, because it had all been eaten by others, but there was still some pottage remaining. Most of the meat had been fished out of the pottage before Tomos' arrival, but he salvaged bits of bacon and cabbage and was thankful, though still hungry after he had supped.

A chaff-filled pallet laid out on the taproom floor was all that was available, but within minutes of his reclining, Tomos was fast asleep.

27

When they got back to The Feathers in Ledbury late that afternoon, Tom and Tamsin announced that they were going to explore the town and would not be joining Sean and Eddie for dinner at the hotel. After quickly washing and changing they went out or, as Sean put it, "escaped into the town."

Relieved to be temporarily free of Sean's obsessions and Eddie's incomprehensible speech, they wandered around the quaint streets. They saw the extraordinarily well preserved market hall, built on stilts in the 17th century, and the ancient town clock, a stone tower with an ornate, top-heavy roof, which dominated the main street. Looking around, they were amazed to see how many half-timbered buildings there were in the town, and realized why this part of Herefordshire was known as "black and white country".

Further along the main street, which was called The Homend, they found an Italian restaurant, The Olive Tree, went in and found a nice table by the window.

"You were hard on Sean today," said Tamsin as they were looking at the menus.

"I know, but if someone doesn't rein him in, I think he's going to flip his lid."

"Even so, it doesn't seem quite fair to attack his God so viciously."

"Well, that's it isn't it? This character from four hundred years ago has become his God. Don't you think that's weird, not to mention unhealthy?"

"I guess, but you can see why he has become so immersed in Dr. Dee. He was a remarkable man."

"Remarkable, yes but not infallible. And certainly not perfect."

"If the argument had continued, what else would you have said to Sean about Dee?"

"For starters, when Talbot—or Kelly or whatever he called himself—wanted to cause trouble because he couldn't get exactly what he wanted, he'd refuse to co-operate and wouldn't do all the angel nonsense for Dee. So then Dee got his little kid, his own son, trying to force him to become a medium. Of course, it was bound to be a complete failure because the original stuff with Talbot was a hoax. Apparently, the little kid was scared shitless."

"Not so good." Tamsin frowned. "But what about all Dee's accomplishments?"

"Sean talks about all the accolades he got in foreign countries, but he doesn't ever mention the times he was laughed out of town, and ordered to move on."

"Where was this?"

"Europe. They tried to do their song and dance in a number of places, but the locals saw right through it. In fact, in Prague, a declaration was issued against him, forbidding his entry on the grounds that he was an undesirable."

"Are you done now, because the waitress wants to take our order."

"I'm just getting warmed up, but you're right, we should eat. What're you having?"

"I'll have the prosciutto with melon to start," said Tamsin, "and then the trout with prawns in a lemon-garlic sauce."

"And for you, sir?" asked the waitress.

"I think I will start with the calamari with sweet chili dip, and for my main course, the chicken and mushrooms in Marsala sauce.

And bring us a bottle of the Soave Classico, please."

"Certainly, sir."

"Alright. Go on," Tamsin said. "You're obviously determined to get it all off your chest and it would be better to say it to me than to Sean. Given his present state, I doubt it would do any good, anyway."

"I just want to put some perspective on the subject," insisted Tom. "I mean, Sean goes on about all the wonderful offers Dee got for hundreds of pounds, but he doesn't say anything about the times Dee couldn't even pay his bills. Even after his friends—and he didn't have that many—came up with five hundred pounds, he still had to hawk his books in the streets to cover his debts."

"You're making me feel sorry for him now," Tamsin said.

"When he signed as warden of Manchester College he called himself John Dee M.A., so he wasn't even a doctor after all!"

"So not a superman, but, it would seem, a normal human being."

"After the Queen died in 1603, he petitioned King James to put him on trial for witchcraft. He had led such a weird and kooky life and was the subject of so much gossip, he figured this was the only way he could clear his name."

"What did the king do?"

"Rejected it out of hand. It was what a modern court would say was 'frivolous and vexatious'."

"Alright, Tom. You've made your point, although I can't for the life of me see why you've been going on like this. Sean is supposed to be your friend."

"He is. I just don't want him to get carried away."

"So you said."

"Before we go back, let's go and have a pint."

"Not for me," Tamsin said. "You go ahead. I'm worn out. I'm going back to the hotel and straight to sleep."

Confused, and with a sense of having done something wrong but not knowing what, Tom took this as some kind of an instruction, so he silently accompanied her back to The Feathers.

Then he wandered along the street until he came to a pub called The Talbot, so he went in and sat on a stool at the bar. He had a pint of Henry's IPA, then one of 6X Original and became mildly drunk.

"We don't get many Americans drinking real ale," said the bar-maid. "They usually say it's too warm and doesn't have enough fizz."

"I'm, not an American. I'm a Canadian and I like this beer a lot."

"Glad you enjoy it," she said. "There's lots more where that came from."

As he sauntered back to the hotel, Tom had a tremendous sense of foreboding, which he could neither identify nor explain. He just knew something was going to happen. Changes of some kind were in the air.

XXVIII

Maelgwn was whinnying and snorting in the stable when Tomos visited him before breaking his fast. He was indeed a magnificent animal, and Tomos was proud to be his owner, and even prouder to have been the one to have bred and reared him.

Maelgwn's eyes were bright and his coat was gleaming. The stallion was in fine fettle and anxious to be on the road.

"Amynedd fy harddwch," said Tomos. "I shall not be above twenty minutes while I snatch something to eat. I see you have had your meal; now I must have mine."

He re-entered the inn, sat and partook of the bread, cheese and ale which the innkeeper's wife put before him. It was plain food, indeed, even the cheese was of the cheapest, hardest kind, but he made good work of it and was sure it would see him through until nightfall.

While Tomos would fain as go to the stars than let Maelgwn be without sustenance at midday, at which time he would stop and let him graze, he had different rules for himself. He believed that the less food, drink and rest a man had upon the road, the better off he would be and, as consequence, would allow nothing to pass his lips until suppertime. The only exception to this rule was if they happened to encounter a spring or a fresh babbling brook, in which case he might wet his whistle.

He saddled Maelgwn and carefully checked his baggage and equipment. He took especial care to examine the pouch beneath the saddle which contained the authorities and articles of safe passage. Obtained from magistrates between Sussex and Wales, these were his most treasured possessions, because in Queen Elizabeth's England it was not legal to travel abroad without permission. If these documents should be lost or stolen, Tomos could be thrown in jail and his horse forfeit.

Today, they would be making for Marlborough, some thirty miles away. They would follow the main Bristol road out of Basingstoke as far as Kingsclere, take the lesser road to Sydmonton, then strike across the country through Combe, Buttermere and Shalborne until they met the Marlborough road. They would of necessity have to pass through a portion of Savernake Forest—a place known for its gnarled and twisted trees, and was thought by many to be bewitched—but he prayed he would not meet any of the Queen's agents. If perchance he did, then he prayed even harder that the agents would be honest and not corrupt.

Just as they were branching off at Kingsclere, Tomos spied a ragged fellow who was haranguing a group of ignorant, ill-dressed peasants. He reined in and halted at the rear of the small crowd, listening to the man's sermon.

At length, the fellow ended his exhortations and the crowd dispersed.

"Good morrow, preacher," said Tomos, dismounting.

"Good morrow, sir. May God look kindly on your journey."

"I thank 'ee, but I must say something to you in great earnest."

"Pray. what is that, sir?"

"I care not what God a man worships, but in these times it is folly to preach according to the old way."

"I cannot put aside my beliefs. What was good in Queen Mary's time must be good enough for me now."

"But don't 'ee know that recusants can be punished?"

"I do, sir, but I have no property they can take from me."

"But you could be imprisoned. Do you have a license to preach?"

"I do not, sir."

"Then I pity thee if you should fall foul of The Watch. You would be charged for two offences. You would likely die in jail."

"I thank 'ee for your concern, but I must do what my conscience dictates."

"Very well. I wish you well. I have far to go and must be aroint."

He veered Maelgwn westwards and felt the hot sun on the back of his neck. A few hours later, near Farracombe, they were forced into the ditch by a peasant driving a large flock of sheep to Kingsclere Market. While the sheep looked healthy and well fed, Tomos noted that the drover was pale and wasted, and was dressed very poorly.

When the sheep had passed, Maelgwn clambered out of the ditch and shook himself.

Tomos had noticed on his way down from Wales to Sussex that the general situation of the rural population was one of demoralization and poverty, they appearing to be glum, run-down and undernourished. He also saw that some villages had but a few houses, while others had been abandoned entirely.

He would have thought the effects of the Great Plague some two hundred years ago would have so diminished the population that agricultural workers would be in demand and could command good wages. But he saw little sign of this and attributed it to landowners shifting from growing crops to raising sheep as the appetite for wool increased both in Britain and abroad. This must have meant that peasants had lost their livelihoods when the lands they had farmed were fenced off to graze sheep.

Those who were driven from the land into the towns and cities, Tomos thought, would face an even grimmer life, as the new cloth-making industry was not in need of unskilled workers.

Even though they were heading across country towards Marlborough, it did not at all mean that they were travelling in a straight line. The ancient Romans, who occupied the British Isles for over three hundred and sixty years, built roads as straight as a die, but there were no old Roman roads hereabouts and the country lanes wandered about incoherently. Tomos knew by the sun that, while generally heading west, they had gone to the south and back to the north many times.

The sun had almost set when they entered the ancient town of Marlborough, which had been occupied by many men from the stone age to the present. Tomos had heard that the Saxons had called the place Merleberge, said to have meant the hill where the beautiful, bright blue gentian grows.

Both he and Maelgwn were hungry and tired and were thankful to turn into the stables at The Marlborough Inn. He unharnessed the horse, brushed him down and gave him a good stack of fresh hay, and a little corn and rye in a leather bucket.

Once inside, Tomos called for a gill of ale, the first liquid to pass his lip since sunrise. He was fortunate that they had a spare bed for him in the traveller's room, but as long as he kept his dagger at the ready, Tomos did not mind sharing, despite the assured company of fleas in the night.

Fish was being served tonight, it having been made compulsory on Wednesdays, Fridays, and Saturdays some twenty years ago by order of the Queen. Since it was some sixty miles to the sea by the shortest route—some two days' ride—the fish was of no identifiable variety and was stinking to high Heaven. So Tomos mashed it into the pottage of turnips and oats and thereby disguised its unpleasantness.

After a further gill of ale, he repaired to the back room and was asleep within minutes.

29

They gathered for breakfast at The Feathers at eight that morning. Sean barely grunted a salutation as they sat down at the table. They buried their faces in the menus trying to choose from the many tempting items.

Suddenly realizing that something was different, Tamsin looked up.

"Where's Eddie?"

"Gone." Sean said.

"Gone?" Tom echoed.

"Yes."

"What do you mean 'gone'?" Tom said. "Gone where?"

"Don't know."

"Don't know? Didn't he say where he was going when he said goodbye?"

"Didn't say goodbye."

"Sean," Tamsin said in a serious tone, "did you see him go? Or did he just disappear like a thief in the night?"

"Disappeared like a thief in the night," Sean repeated.

"You mean he actually stole something?"

"Nothing of material value." Sean sighed and put down his menu. "Alright. He was there when I went to sleep, but he was gone when I woke up. As far as I could tell, none of my possessions were missing. End of story. Satisfied? Happy now?"

"How extraordinary!" Tamsin said.

"You must have had words," said Tom. "Was there an argument last night?"

"There was no argument," Sean said. "I had no idea he was going to leave. He gave me no reason to suppose he would. But he has gone. There's no doubt about that."

"Did he even leave a note?" Tamsin asked.

"Eddie was hardly the literary type. No, there was no note."

"What an asshole!"

"Please don't abuse him," said Sean sternly. "He was a friend of mine."

"Sean, you only knew him for a few days. He wasn't really a friend," said Tamsin.

"He was a friend!" Sean insisted indignantly. "If he had to take off, he must have had a good reason."

"Well, if he's gone, he's gone. There's nothing we can do about it. We can hardly go to the police and file a missing person's report," said Tom.

"No, we can't do that."

"So, let's eat. The waitress wants to take our order."

They ordered their breakfast. This time Tom had the eggs Benedict, Tamsin the full English, and Sean a bacon and sausage sandwich. The men ordered coffee while Tamsin had tea. They ate in silence for several minutes.

"Do we have a plan for today, Tom?" Sean asked.

"Yes, subject to your approval, of course."

"Let's hear it."

"We take the A438 to Hereford, where we take a look at the cathedral."

"Oooh, good!" said Tamsin.

"If it doesn't take too long," Sean said.

"I would think two hours, tops, maybe less. That alright?"

"I guess so. Then what?"

"We go back on the A438 to Staunton on Wye, where we branch off for a few miles."

"Why?" demanded Sean.

"To see Arthur's Stone."

"Arthur's Stone!" echoed Tamsin, "How do they know King Arthur threw it?"

"He didn't throw it," Tom said with a chuckle. "Nobody threw it. It's a Neolithic chambered tomb. The stones are much too big for even twenty men to throw, let alone one. It's supposed to be a fine example because you can see all the stones. Other similar tombs are partially covered with earth."

"Why are we going there? It's way before our period."

"Yes, how old is it, Tom?" Tamsin asked.

"About five thousand years old. The point is that Arthur's Stone is exactly equidistant from Llanbister and Upton on Severn, so I would say Dr. Dee is bound to have visited the site."

"Exactly equidistant?" Sean asked, now excited.

"Well within less than a quarter of a mile."

"Wow, that's close enough for me. It must be significant. For sure we'll go there! Then what?"

"Then we leave the A438 after Letton, and take the A4111 past Spond to Kington—"

"Don't you just love the place names?" Tamsin interjected.

"—Then we head for New Radnor and join the A44, and then take the A483 to Llanbister. Before we get to Llanbister, we should go to see Abbeycwmhir –which means abbey in the long valley, and is the remains of a Cistercian religious house built in the twelfth century."

"Dr. Dee would have been there many times," said Sean with complete certainty.

"Exactly," Tom said. "I have booked us into The Lion. It's not the same kind of place as The Feathers, but apparently it is excellent, though down to earth."

"What time should we get there?"

"It's hard to say, but I wouldn't bet on getting there much before late afternoon."

"Alright," Sean said. "What about tomorrow?"

"Tomorrow we go to see Nant y Groes."

"Nanty y Groes!" Sean echoed.

"Isn't that where Dr. Dee was born?" Tamsin asked.

"No, he was born in London. Remember that his dad, Roland, was a courtier to Henry VIII," explained Tom, "but Nant y Groes Hall was built by his grandfather, Beddw Dee. I read that the antiques from the hall were auctioned a couple of years ago for forty-five thousand pounds."

"Yes," said Sean, his eyes alight. "Dr. Dee kept his connection with the area. He said that he was descended from Rhodri Mawr, Rhodri the Great, the ninth century king of Gwynedd."

"Gwynedd? Isn't that a woman's name?"

"It is a contraction of 'Gwyn, bendigedig, hapusrwydd', which means 'white, blessed and happiness', so it is a common name for girls. But in this case it was the name for the northwest kingdom in Wales."

"And what does Nant y Groes mean in English?" asked Tamsin.

"It means 'the stream of the cross'."

"Oh, how nice! Will we be able to see the hall?"

"Only from the outside. It's privately owned."

"That's too bad. But we must see it," said Sean. "What else is on tomorrow's program?"

"On our way to Nant y Groes, apparently there is a lovely old church, St Mary's, and a holy well."

"A holy well! Can we leave prayers there on bits of paper?" asked Tamsin.

"I don't know. I shouldn't think so. I imagine they would regard that as littering. You can say some prayers if you want to. And after we take a peek at Nant y Groes we go a few miles to a village called Whitton where you can see Offa's Dyke."

"What on earth is that?" Tamsin asked.

"It's a gigantic earthwork," said Tom, turning the page in his guide book, "Built by Offa. the Anglo-Saxon king of Mercia—that's roughly the central part of England—in the eighth century, as a boundary between Wales and Mercia."

"You can bet Dr. Dee went there." Sean was definite.

"I've been reading quite a bit about it from various sources," said Tom. "The dyke was a ditch which was dug on the Welsh side to make a bank on the English side, which in places is eight feet high. It ran for a hundred and seventy seven miles. It was sixty-five-feet wide."

"Did it keep the Welsh out?" Sean asked.

"I don't see how it could. I mean, how many men would it take to man a bank a hundred and seventy seven miles long? It may have been more of a status symbol. Offa was flexing his muscles."

"Let's see," said Sean, taking out his pen and scribbling on the back of the menu. "If they placed one soldier every one hundred feet, I figure they would need over nine thousand men. That's a huge chunk of your army to tie up in one place."

"Have there been any archaeological excavation on the dyke?" Tamsin inquired.

"Yes, quite a bit, apparently, but most have only discovered how it was constructed. One curious item I came across was that back in the 1970s a Nova Scotian funded excavations here."

"Really?"

"Yes, some fellow called Akerman."

"Well, we'd better get on the road," said Sean.

XXX

After leaving Marlborough, Tomos and Maelgwn were bound for Gloucester, an ancient city founded by the Romans, which lay on the River Severn between the Cotswold Hills to the east and the Royal Forest of Dean to the west. This was to be the longest leg of their journey, at some forty miles, and, despite the beast being in high health and spirits, Tomos was somewhat concerned that Maelgwn might find it too much for him.

Their journey would take them north through the villages of Ogbourne St. Andrew and Ogbourne St. George to Suindune—meaning *the hill of pigs*. Tomos had heard some talk about the local lord of Suindune, Sir Richard Goddard, who was said to be overly diligent about applying and enforcing the laws of vagrancy and sumptuary. So he was determined to give the place a wide berth and circumvent the town by way of Liddington and Wanborough.

Then they would have what Tomos hoped would be a very pleasant ride through the quaint, yellow-stoned, tiny Cotswold villages of Cricklade, Driffield, Stratton, Middle Duntisbourne, Duntisbourne Leer, Winstone, Elkstone and Birdlip. He had always found the folk thereabout to be friendly and welcoming and, apart from the occasional fellow who had too much drink taken, to be gentle people and not given to harrying travellers.

It was the kind of day when a man knows not what to put on his back from one hour to the next. There was a goodish sun, but clouds would blow over it and a wind would come up, making it cold until the morning had become noon.

Tomos pulled on his jerkin over his doublet and decided to let Maelgwn pace for some miles, something the animal loved to do when he was allowed. Were he permitted to pace for too long, it would certainly tire him out for the longer journey, and they might not be able to reach their destination.

As they approached the Ogbourne villages, Tomos looked back and could just discern away to the west of Marlborough that strange Silbury Hill, whose date or purpose no man could explain. He had heard his cousin, John, say that buried deep inside the hill was a life-sized gold statue of King Sil, or Zel, sitting astride a horse. Sil was said to be of the Dal Riata of Munster, though what he might be doing in Wiltshire remained a mystery, and he was not recorded in the recitation of English monarchs.

Others repeated the legend that the Devil was flying over with a monstrous bag of soil to deposit on Marlborough, but that it slipped from his grip and fell upon the field where it now lay.

That afternoon the clouds dispersed and the sun now shone without let or hindrance, so Tomos removed his jerkin and stowed it in his pack. They had passed Wanborough and were now approaching Blunsdon St. Andrew, and Tomos was congratulating himself for having avoided Suindune and the supposedly overly-zealous Sir Richard.

But as they were skirting a wood and heading along the banks of a rene, or artificial brook, Tomos spied a stern figure riding towards them, accompanied by another armed with a pike. Apart from the fact that the first man was mounted, which few were, his appearance announced that he was clearly someone of importance, and superior to the other fellow.

"Good den," said the first man brusquely.

"May God give you a good day, sir." Tomos was careful to be polite.

"Who are you?" the man demanded.

"I am Tomos Jones of Porth Farm, near Bwlch y Sarnau, of the parish of the same name, in the county of Radnor. I ask as much of you, sir."

"I am Robert Harrison, Sheriff of the County of Wiltshire, if you must know, and I am given wide powers to execute my duties. How do you come to be dressed as you do?"

"I can produce documents to show that I am of that class which, under the Queen's sumptuary laws, is entitled to wear a doublet and the other garments which I now bear and carry with me."

"Show me the documents."

"I am more than willing for you to see them, sir, but they shall not leave my hands"

"Very well. Produce them."

Tomos removed the leather pouch from its hiding place and held out, but did not release, the papers for the Sheriff to view.

That gentleman scrutinized them closely, then nodded. "I crave your pardon, Master Jones. I see you are entitled to your dress according to law. But the Queen is strict about these matters, so must we be, too. She has decreed that every person shall be dressed appropriate to his or her class."

"I comprehend fully, sir. I am sensible that you have your duties to perform. I thank you for your kindness."

"Whither are you bound, Master Jones?"

"I look to stop at Gloucester tonight, and tomorrow on to Hereford."

"That is a long way to travel, but I see you have a fine, healthy mount who is equal to the task."

"Indeed he is, sir. I raised him myself from birth. I call him Maelgwn."

"That is a name most strange to my ears. Is it Welsh?"

"It is. It is the name of an ancient prince of Gwynedd in north Wales."

"It is fitting for such a fine animal. I must bid you farewell for I have much work to do hereabouts."

"Good day to you, sir. I am glad we were well met."

The Sheriff turned his horse and started to make away, then reined it in and called back to Tomos. "It quite escaped my mind, Master Jones, but I should advise you not to go into Gloucester to-night."

"For what reason?"

"Rioting. There have been food riots there for some days, so there is great unrest in the city."

"Marry, that is bad news. I thank 'ee for your advice and will follow it. I am somewhat acquainted with the village of Coberly. I shall head there and will avoid Gloucester completely."

"That is meet. I know Coberly. Shall you board at the Seven Springs Inn?"

"I shall."

"Then I wish you well, Master Jones."

"May God also go with you, Sheriff."

Tomos watched the Sheriff and his servant go into the wood, allowed Maelgwn to graze on the good grass for a few more minutes, and then clucked the horse to amble onward.

The day was exceeding fine now, with the sun beating down upon them. All clouds had disappeared and the sky was a clear blue from horizon to horizon, west to east. As Tomos had expected, the ride through the Cotswolds was a great pleasure and, as they went through the villages with flowers growing up the stone walls of the houses, they were hailed by the inhabitants they passed.

Just before Cockleford, Maelgw threw a shoe, so Tomos gently walked him into the village. To his great fortune, the first person he saw was the blacksmith, one Jos Bennett, who promptly attended to his horse's problem. Tomos paid the good man, regretfully declined his invitation to take a tankard of cider with him, and went about his business.

Again, it was well after dark when they arrived at the inn at Coberly, but Tomas was lucky to find there were no other visitors and that he could have a bedchamber to himself.

Further good news awaited him when he came in from attending to Maelgwn's needs. The landlady, a cheery, friendly body, informed him that she was roasting a goose and, if he did but wait a half hour, he could freely partake of it. Needing no second bidding, he washed and cleaned himself, took a gill of her best ale, and sat down to a feast.

The mistress joined him for supper and they enjoyed the glistening brown goose with turnips, cabbage and good gravy.

Weary, but satisfied and well fed, Tomos retired to his bedchamber and was dreaming of dusty lanes, thatched cottages, and flowers as soon as he had lowered his head onto the good round log which the mistress had been kind enough to wrap in a soft towel.

31

When they reached Hereford and negotiated the streets until they could find a place to park, they went straight to the cathedral. The magnificent old building was dedicated to St. Mary the Virgin and St. Ethelbert the King (whom they later discovered was murdered by Offa, builder of the dyke), and was commenced in the eleventh century. They stayed much longer at the cathedral than they had planned, not because of Tom or Tamsin, but because Sean became obsessed with some of the treasures on display and finally had to be pried away.

They admired the huge windows, the spacious nave and a wonderful nineteenth century Wills organ which, fortunately for them, was being played as they stood under it. They found the playing thunderously loud, but amazing and uplifting as it filled every corner of the edifice. Its lower notes—as Sean put it—shook the ground under their feet and stirred fires in their bellies.

What really captured Sean's attention was the "Chain Library", so-called because the books were secured from theft by chains attaching them to their shelves. He became riveted by two of the world's most extraordinary documents, the Mappa Mundi of 1300 and a copy of the 1217 Magna Carta, both of which he was sure would have preoccupied Dr. Dee.

The Magna Carta supposedly represented a rapprochement between King John and rebellious barons, and pledged protection for the barons from illegal imprisonment; and affirmed church rights, limits on feudal payments to the king, and access to prompt justice. Four copies survive of those made in 1215, and four of those fabricated in 1217. This was one of the latter.

Sean was enraptured, and spent many minutes staring at the faded, browning document and then reading its translation into modern English.

But what gripped him even more was the Mappa Mundi, one of the earliest maps of the world and the largest of the medieval maps. About five feet tall, it showed Jerusalem in the middle of a circle the Garden of Eden, and the British Isles in a corner, as well as elephants and camels.

"Dr. Dee must have been as happy as a pig in shit here," enthused Sean.

"I'm sure you're right," said Tom.

"Amazing! Amazing!" Sean repeated. "What do you think, Tamsin?"

"It is remarkable that something on a single sheet of vellum could have survived for over seven hundred years."

"Sean," said Tom, "If we want to stick to our schedule, we'd better go."

"Yes, of course. In a few minutes."

Leaving Sean to pore over the Mappa, Tom and Tamsin went to look at the outside of the cathedral. Eventually, Sean came out and they left to find their car.

In less than half an hour they were at Arthur's Stone, a monument actually consisting of as many as twenty stones. There were a number of smaller, upright stones supporting a giant capstone which must have weighed over twenty tonnes. A stone to the north had indentations in it which, Tom said with a snicker, were made by the king's elbows when he knelt down to pray.

"I still don't understand," Tamsin said. "If this was erected five thousand years ago, what has it got to do with King Arthur."

"Nothing," Tom said. "There are hundreds of sites all over the country, from Scotland to Cornwall, which are said to be associated with Arthur, but nothing has ever been found to prove it."

"Not found yet," Sean said firmly.

"First, they have to find some evidence that Arthur really existed."

"How could they do that?" Tamsin asked.

"They couldn't unless some kind of written document came to light."

"And which also said he was a king?"

"Exactly. And we know there was never an Arthur who was king of England, and if he was a king, we have no idea of what province or country."

"The important thing is," said Sean, "that this chambered tomb is exactly halfway between Upton and Nant y Groes, and that can't be an accident!"

"But Sean," Tom said, "this was built thousands of years before Upton and Nant y Groes. Are you suggesting that those two places sprang up where they did as a result of deliberate design?"

"I'm not sure what I'm saying, but I am sure that Dr. Dee spent many hours on this very spot. I feel him more strongly than anywhere else we have been."

Sean walked around the site, arms outstretched, muttering, "Yes, yes, yes," to himself. At length, he reluctantly got into the car.

An hour later they were heading up the A44, a pretty road through the splendid Welsh countryside of rivers, hills, farmhouses and millions of sheep. They turned off onto the busy, and not so nice, A483, the twisting main road to the north.

Within a few miles, Tom saw the sign to Abbeycwmhir, but too late to turn, so he had to pull into a farm gate and wait until traffic subsided before executing a quick about turn.

They parked the car and walked to the site of the abbey, which had been a Cistercian monastery, founded in 1176 by the Welsh prince Cadwallon ap Madog. Most of the existing walls were not much more than waist high, and only in places more than six feet, but the building had covered an enormous area, almost as much as some cathedrals.

The site lay in an idyllic location alongside a river called the Nant Clywedog, which itself was in a long, quiet, green valley bordered by tall trees. So long as they were not disturbed by marauding soldiers, Tom thought, the monks could have had a decent life here, drawing their water and fish from the river and tending their cattle and sheep on the extensive pastures.

Sean wandered off on his own while Tamsin and Tom sat on a wall, enjoying the sunshine. The tension Tom had felt between them in Ledbury seemed to have dissipated, and he was glad to see her so apparently happy and carefree again. However, he thought he discerned that she had made some kind of decision, though what it was he could not guess.

A wild cry from Sean brought them over to a spot against the east wall. There was a plaque indicating the burial place of Llywelyn ap Gruffudd, or Llywelyn the Last, who died in 1282. He was, so the inscription on the stone told them, one of the last native and independent princes of Wales, before its being overrun by Edward I of England.

"We are in the presence of royalty," said Sean solemnly. "I feel the doctor's presence also. He must have made many visits to this place."

"Wow!" said Tamsin. "A prince's grave."

"I wonder if he really is under there," Tom asked.

"O, ye of little faith!" Sean said.

"Yes, always the skeptic, Tom," Tamsin added.

"Just trying to keep a sense of proportion."

"Right, enough proportion," said Sean. "On to The Lion."

In less than twenty minutes they pulled into the car park of The Lion and were cheerfully welcomed by Ray and Janet Thomas, the proprietors. Janet told them she was descended from Elystan Glodrydd, the eleventh-century ruler of the cantref of Builth in central Wales, and was therefore a relative of the founder of the abbey they had just visited.

They checked in and were assigned rooms in the hotel, Sean getting the Maelienydd Room and Tom and Tamsin the Dorddu Room. They agreed to meet in the bar at six for pre-dinner drinks.

XXXII

The next morning was not fair, and brought gray clouds and fine rain, but this was not what worried Tomos about this, his fourth day on the road to home. He knew that both he and Maelgwn could suffer to bear all but the most extreme weather, and the fact that this would be the shortest leg of their journey at thirty miles was in their favour.

But Tomos knew that unless he made a wider sweep through Much Markle, Putley, Trumpet and Lugwardine, an additional fifteen miles, he would have to go through the Royal Forest of Dean in order to reach Hereford.

There were two routes he could take through the forest. The first, slightly longer, led from Perrystone Hill through Sollers Hope, and Mordiford, entering Hereford along the north bank of the River Wye. The second was by way of Ross on Wye, Birdstow, Dadnow, Red Rail and Little Dewchurch, and into the city on the Hoarwithy Road.

Tomos knew not which of these would be for the best, so he was determined to wait until he reached Boxbush or Lea and make up his mind at that juncture.

He took care of Malegwn's needs and had a hearty breakfast of bread, cold leftover goose and cider. He told the landlady to expect him again in five days, at which time he would be accompanied by two servants, two horses, and a carriage, on his way back to Sussex to collect Thomasina. He then bid farewell to the hospitable mistress of the Seven Springs Inn, who had been kind to him and had given him the best eating of his journey to date.

Although wet and windy and somewhat muddy under hoof, the going to Boxbush was uneventful, and Tomos rode on slowly to Lea, trying to decide which route to take through the forest. Just as he was approaching the village, he heard the sound of jingling bells, laughter and singing.

Rounding the bend in the road, he came upon a group of about ten men who, from all appearances, were a band of travelling players. As he rode up they hailed him in a cheerful manner, so he reined Maelgwn in and stopped.

The group's leader, a man of about forty, stepped forward. "Good morrow, master."

"Well met, sir."

"I am Ned Raynolds, at your service."

"And I am Tomos Jones. I discern you be travelling players unless I am mistaken, sir."

"Indeed, you are not mistaken, sir. We specialize in singing, reciting and the music of instruments, also presenting plays when we can attract the citizenry to hear them."

"I marvel at any who have the talents to perform before others. It is something I could not do, myself."

"It is my experience, sir, that many a man can perform, if only indifferently, if he has enough ale taken or is prevailed upon by a convivial company."

"Marry, you could be right on that! Do you mind telling me where you are bound, Master Raynolds?"

"I do not. We are bound for the fair city of Hereford and hope to arrive afore nightfall."

"I am exceeding glad to hear that," said Tomos, "for, should you permit it, I would travel along with you as, being alone, I fear to travel in the forest."

"You are right to do so. As they do say, there is safety in numbers. Come you, and meet our company."

Tomos dismounted and followed Ned into the camp, where he was introduced to each member of the society of performers. There were twins, Ralph and Cyril, aged about thirty; Silas, a jolly fat man of fifty; John, Robert and Arthur, all earnest looking fellows of some five and twenty years; and two who were scarcely more than boys, being only seventeen or so.

The first had but the down upon his lip, with a large nose and hair upon his shoulders. The second had frizzled hair, but a wispy moustache and sparkling brown eyes. Both lads gave him the wide, genuine smiles of youths upon an adventure.

"This is Will Shakespeare," said Ned, indicating the former. "He is with us for a brief spell of freedom before he is to be wed in a few months' time. He is a Warwickshire boy. This here is Kit Marlowe, a Kentish lad, who is taking time from his studies at Cambridge and thence to become a man of the cloth."

"I am happy to make the acquaintance of both young gentlemen," said Tomos, "and look forward to seeing them perform."

"They are both full of the Devil." Ned said. "Marry, I swear they do more performing off the stage than on it!"

The youths laughed, and ran off pushing and bumping into one another.

"Master Raynolds, which route shall we take through the forest?"

"I thought to go by way of Ross and the Hoarwithy Road."

"Why that one rather than the other through Perystone and

Modiford?"

"Both routes have their advantages and drawbacks, as I see it. The one is a deal longer, but Royal servants are there seen less commonly. The way through Ross is much frequented by forest officials, but is shorter and should bring us to Hereford before nightfall."

"And you think, Master Raynolds, that due to our numbers the agents might be less likely to try to take advantage of us."

"That is my mind, yes."

"Well, sir, I should be happy to travel with you and I hope you are right that we will fare well."

"We shall be glad of your company Master Jones."

Raynolds turned to the company. "Let us move forward! Who shall give us a song as we go?"

"I will," Silas called out, taking up his lute. "'Tis but a short one."

> *My beloved has gone,*
> *Alas, why is she so?*
> *And I am so sore bound*
> *I may not come her to,*
> *She hath mine heart in hold*
> *Wherever she ride or go,*
> *With true love a thousand fold.*

"If all your company performs as well as Silas, I foresee you shall be a success in Hereford and will make much money," said Tomos.

"I trust you have the power of prophecy, Master Jones," said Ned. "You shall hear much more as we go along. To keep these fellows from singing and reciting would require an army! Ralph,

Cyril: Let us have one from you!"

Cyril tuned up his viol and Ralph fingered a small bagpipe.

"We shall need you all in this," said Ralph, "and your cornet, Robert."

> *Summer is acoming in,*
> *Loud sing cuckoo!*
> *Groweth seed and bloweth mead,*
> *And springeth the wood now,*
> *Sing cuckcoo!*
> *Ewe bleateth after lamb,*
> *Lows both the calf and cow,*
> *Bullock leaps and farts,*
> *Merry sing Cuckoo!*
> *Well singest thou cuckoo:*
> *Ne'er cease thou never now!*

"Well done, lads!" said Ned. "That is the oldest song which is known to us, Master Jones. We believe it comes to us from Norman times, or maybe even earlier."

"I have a song," spake up Kit Marlowe. "'Twas given to me by Master William Byrd, whom I lately met at Cambridge. I believe he has not yet published it."

> *The nightingale so pleasant and so gay*
> *In greenwood groves delights to make his dwelling.*
> *In fields to fly chanting his roundelay.*
> *At liberty. Against the cage rebelling;*
> *But my poor heart with sorrows over swelling,*
> *Through bondage vile, binding my freedom short,*

No pleasure takes in these sports excelling,
Nor in his song receiveth no comfort.

"Marry, but I am being well entertained today," said Tomos, "and look, 'tis clear that Maelgwn likes it well, too. How about you, young Shakespeare? Shall you not give us something?"

"Alas, sir, I am no singer, but I will recite a poem for you," said the lad. "It comes from the pen of Master John Skelton who was lately writing in King Henry's time:"

My name is Parrot a bird of Paradise,
By nature devised with diverse delicate spice,
Till Euphrates, that flood, driveth me into Inde;
Where men of that country by fortune me find,
And send me to great ladies of estate;
Then Parrot must have an almond or a date.

By and by, they came to the little town of Ross on Wye, perched upon the bank of a greatly winding river from which many goodly salmon are fished; and crossing the bridge there, they entered the Royal Forest of Dean.

Kit and Will seized the opportunity to go swimming in the river for a short while as the horses were being watered and rested. Ned and Tomos looked southward over the many bends in the river, observing in the distance the stout castle of Goodrich, the stronghold of the powerful Talbot family.

Ned called them to gather themselves together and to set forward once more, which, after some mischief from Kit and Will, they eventually did. The going was good, the weather brightened up and the day was without noteworthy event until they came to the village of Dadnor.

There they spied ahead a richly apparelled man on a white mare in the company of five lesser fellows, all of whom were armed and had a threatening look.

The man on the white mare spurred his mount into the road and held up his hand. "Halt in Her Majesty's name!"

They did as they were commanded and Ned and Tomos rode forward to meet them, doffing their hats and bowing in their saddles.

"Good morrow, my lord," said Tomos.

"Good morrow. I am Henry Herbert, Earl of Pembroke. Warden of Her Majesty's Forest of Dean, and these are my verderers who are charged with enforcing the Forest rules. I must ask you who you are and where you are going."

Tomos told him who he was and presented his papers of passage, whereupon the earl examined Ned, instructing his men to do likewise with the assembled company. At length, each man was questioned, required to produce his laissez passer, and the wagons and carts were searched.

"Very well," said Earl Henry at long last, "you shall pass. I am satisfied you mean no ill, carry no contraband and will not harm any creature in the forest. Nor, I entreat you, are you to remove, for any purpose whatever, any form of wood or tree while you are in the forest. Do you understand?"

"Yes, my lord." Ned and Tomos spake as one.

"In which case, I bid you Godspeed."

The earl lightly whipped his mare and was gone in a cloud of dust in the direction of Ross, his underlings straggling behind him.

Greatly relieved to have passed muster with the Warden, the company pressed on with light hearts, playing their instruments and singing the Earl of Surrey, Henry Howard's famous lines as they went.

> *Set me whereas the sun doth parch the green*
> *Or where his beams do not dissolve the ice*
> *In temperate heat where he is felt and seen;*
> *In present press of people, mad or wise;*
> *Set me in high or yet low degree.*
> *In the longest night or in the shortest day,*
> *In clearest sky or where clouds thickest be,*
> *In lusty youth or when my hairs are grey.*
> *Set me in heaven, in earth, or else in hell:*
> *In hill, or dale, or in the foaming flood;*
> *Thrall or at large alive whereso I dwell,*
> *Sick or in health, in evil frame or good:*
> *Hers will I be, and only with this thought*
> *Content myself although my chance be nought.*

In these high spirits, they approached the Wye at Hereford just as night had fallen. They left the Hoarwithy Road, followed the Ross Road to the bridge, crossed it and then dispersed.

Ned and Tomos took a room at the Black Lion, an ancient inn of medieval foundation which lay in Bridge Street; while Silas, Robert and John sought lodgings in nearby houses. Shakespeare, Marlowe, Arthur and the twins were charged with keeping close eye on the horses and vehicles, and to make shift as best they could by the river bank.

Tomos and Ned each had a gill of cider made from the best Herefordshire apples, and ordered that a leg of hogget be boiled for them along with root vegetables. Despite the warmness of the day, they sat beside a fire and told each other many tales about their greatly varied lives. With their food, they drank the local ale, finding it bitter, fine and satisfying.

Such meat as they did not consume that night, they set aside to break their fast the following day.

XXXIII

Dr. Dee came hurrying up the road from Dropsorrow village in a tempestuous rage. He had received bad news from thence and was cursing the heavens and the stars in the sky. He skittered over the gravelled threshold and stormed into the house, shouting for Talbot to come to him as he went.

The doctor went straight to his study, flung himself into his chair and immediately began to write.

A timid tap on the door announced the arrival of Talbot. "You summoned me, Master?"

"Yes I did, you dog!"

"Master?" Talbot was taken aback by the harshness of his master's words.

"I have just heard from the carter that, in last week's rains, my vital message to the Queen's Secretary of State was lost into the Rother at Coultershaw Bridge!"

"Master, I—"

"You knew of this and did not think to tell me, you knave!"

"I did not think it important at the time I was told it, and then other events put it out of my mind."

"You did not think it important? Not important! It was of vital importance to the nation, to the Queen herself, you wretch!"

"Forgive me, Master—"

"No, I will not forgive you! I have a good mind to dismiss you from my employment. Now, you stand there while I finish this missive."

Talbot stood silently, not daring to make a move as his master enscribed his letter. The steward knew he could not afford to lose his place in Dr. Dee's household, and yet he inwardly seethed with anger. To himself, he vowed an oath that he would make the doctor pay for this indignity; he would make them all pay.

The doctor finished writing, then sealed the letter.

"Take that this instant" he commanded Talbot, "and see to it that it is put into the closest care and not thrown casually on the back of the cart."

"At once, Master," Talbot said sulkily.

"And look you, Talbot: should you fail this time you shall not only be dismissed from my service but I shall see you whipped for your insolence!"

"Yes, Master," Talbot muttered. He turned on heel and ran from the house as fast as his legs would carry him.

34

When Tamsin and Tom came down for breakfast they found Sean slumped at the table, staring at the wall and appearing to be lost in thought.

"Good morning, Sean," said Tamsin, "Did you sleep well?"

"I didn't sleep." Sean replied. "I didn't go to bed. I was up reading."

"Good God. What could you be reading all night?" Tom asked.

"I was reading the script."

"The script? You must have read that thing a hundred times already."

"I see new things in it. I'm always seeing new things."

"Like what?"

"You'll find out. You'll see them…eventually."

"Sounds ominous," said Tamsin.

"Not ominous. Inevitable."

"What do you mean?"

"Nothing. Let it go," Sean said.

Tamsin and Tom glanced at each other, both smelling trouble.

"I receive no credit," said Sean weirdly. "Not that I need constant thanks for my accomplishments, but I deserve the occasional acknowledgment."

"I don't understand," Tamsin said. "Acknowledgment for what accomplishments?"

At that moment, Janet came in to take their breakfast orders.

Both Tom and Tamsin asked for the Full Welsh because Ray had told them that the bacon, sausages and eggs all came from a nearby farmer friend of his.

After pausing for what seemed like an eternity, Sean said he just wanted toast and coffee. "Cut that in three which nature hath made one," he said mysteriously.

Janet looked at the others. Tom and Tamsin both shrugged. Shaking her head, Janet left for the kitchen.

"Sean," Tom said, "what you were talking about before. Were you referring to the expense of this trip? Because if it's an issue, we can cut the whole thing short right now and go home."

"No, no, no. Well, yes. I am bearing the lion's share of the expense."

"I did warn you in Halifax that I would need a small amount of subsidization. You had no problem with it."

"And I am completely freeloading, aren't I?" said Tamsin, "I'll leave today."

"No!" Tom said quickly.

"No. That isn't necessary," Sean said. "I can afford it. But it wouldn't hurt if you mentioned it once in a while."

"Sorry, Sean. It was thoughtless of us. We'll remember in future."

"There is a strange participation between things supernatural and things natural," Sean said cryptically.

"What?"

"All things are connected, animal aspects, anthropological aspects and plant-animal aspects."

"What on earth are you talking about?"

"Who does not understand should either learn, or be silent."

Sean was quiet for a minute or so, then said very quietly, "I won't be denied access."

"Access to what?" Tamsin asked.

"I won't be denied. I won't allow it."

The breakfasts arrived, and Tamsin and Tom tucked in with relish. Sean played with his toast, tearing it into circles and arranging them on his plate.

Uncomfortable with Sean's behaviour, Tom was anxious to change the subject. "Today we go to Pilleth for St Mary's Church and the holy well, Nant y Groes, and Offa's Dyke. Should be a good day."

"And tomorrow?" Sean inquired. "What happens on the morrow, sirrah?"

"Off to the Sussex downs," Tom answered. "It will probably be a long day's drive. And we'll have to go back on the motorways, more's the pity, because I hate them."

"Do you have a route worked out?" Tamsin asked.

"Yeah. I think we'll have to go back past Hereford and pick up the M5 South just north of Tewkesbury," said Tom, consulting the atlas, "then get the M4 East at Bristol, go south on the A33 at Reading and work our way across country to the A3 south and the A272 to just north of Bepton. From there it is only a hop and a skip to Dropborrow."

"Dropborrow?" Sean instantly perked up.

"Yes, it's a tiny village where Dr. Dee lived after they burned his house down at Mortlake. I've booked us into the Wistman Manor. It's in the middle of nowhere. Smack in the heart of the South Downs."

"Excellent," Sean said. "There is nothing that so much beautifies the soul and mind."

After breakfast they drove through the village of Llanbister and along a narrow, winding country lane until they saw the church at Pilleth. They were enchanted by the small, low, white church which, more like a fort than a place of worship, was hunkered down into the landscape.

Inside, the chancel and nave were combined into a single space, and on one side the stone wall was sloping. However, they all thought the holy well was a little disappointing, although Sean lay down alongside it, put his head inside the stone-lined cavity and muttered something the others could not hear.

The visit to Nant y Groes was also somewhat disappointing because the Hall was set back from the road and could only be reached by way of a private lane. Before Tom and Tamsin knew what was happening, Sean ran across the road and was tearing up the private lane, waving his arms and shouting, "I shall not be denied access!"

They watched him go right up to the house and knock on the door. It soon became apparent that nobody was at home, so Sean wandered around the building, peering through the windows.

After half an hour, he came back to the road, clearly invigorated and red-faced, if a little annoyed.

"I should have been granted access," he said under his breath. "I should not have been denied."

They got back in the car and drove a few miles through the little village of Whitton, then pulled into a farmers' gateway to look out over the green undulating fields.

Hereabouts, it was clear that Offa's Dyke was nowhere near as high as the eight feet which they had been led to expect, as both ditch and bank were noticeable but slight. Unbothered, Sean leaped over the gate and went off to the north along the line of the dyke.

Leaning on the five-barred gate, Tom and Tamsin watched him go, running this way and that, and sometimes moving in circles.

"I think he's really flipped his lid now," said Tom.

"Yes. He's getting worse by the day. What was all that weird stuff he was saying?"

"Those are things Dr. Dee said at one time or another."

"He's learned those, along with his lines in the script?"

"It would seem so. I don't mind admitting to you that I am really starting to get worried about him."

"Me too, but there's nothing we can do, is there?"

"I can't think what. I mean, he would never agree to see a doctor."

"No way."

"We'll just have to hope he doesn't deteriorate any further."

XXXV

Tomos rose in the dark and did not disturb Ned to say his goodbyes, as that good fellow was fast asleep and snoring like a tempest. Nor did he partake of the hogget left over from their evening meal, but quietly slipped out of the Black Lion and hastened to the stables. He had settled his account with the landlord before retiring so there was nothing beside Maelgwn's comforts to detain him.

But even that sturdy steed did not received the usual attentions, Tomos putting some feed into a sack and hanging around the animal's neck.

He led the horse out of the yard and some way down Bridge Street before mounting. Then he made his way through the narrow city byways until they reached the Brecon Road, which led to the west. Today would be their longest journey, at over forty miles, so Tomos knew that, even leaving before light, they would not arrive home until well after dark.

He debated whether he should take the lesser road through Credenhill and Mansel Lacey, there to join the Radnor Road at Lyonshall, but he could tell that there had been many rains hereabouts and he feared it would be heavy going, if indeed going there be. Therefore he determined to head for Letton and branch off on the Eardisley road thereafter, and meet the road to Radnor at the ancient Saxon market town of Kington. Once there, he would be in familiar territory and would have half as much distance again to go before reaching Bwlch y Sarnau.

It was unclear what manner of day it would be as it was still dark when they achieved Byford, but by the time they got to Staunton the sun was showing his first rays.

Tomos paused by the roadside to let Maelgwn drink of the brook which ran alongside, while he surveyed the strange earthen mound which had been built there by the olden people. Some said it was linked to that supposed King Arthur, claimed by many people in many places, but Tomos had the habit of listening to all tales and believing none.

They made exceeding good time and came into Kington in the early afternoon. As they left the town on the Crossgates road, Tomos saw ahead a gentleman, probably a merchant of some kind.

As he drew alongside, he hailed him. "Good den, sir. Do you object if I ride with you for a way?"

"I do not, sir. I am Daffydd Roberts and I am bound for Llanfair-ym-Muallt."

"Alas, then we shall not have each other's company for long, as I have to leave this road and go onto the one to Llanbister. Tomos Jones, at your service, sir."

"You are a merchant too, sir?"

"Nay, I am a farmer and land owner. At Bwlch y Sarnau."

"Ah. I should have guessed by your steed. A mightier creature I never saw."

"He is a blessing and worth his weight in gold." Tomos bent over and stroked Maelgwn's neck. "What is your trade, sir?"

"I deal in quarried stone, which I mine at Llanelwedd and sell to such as can afford to build in the substance. Churches, cities, Lords and the like."

"A noble profession. Did you business in Kington?"

"The church needs some repairs and they asked me if I could provide the stone at a stated price."

"And could you?"

"Alas, no. Were I to accept, I would be losing money. I cannot afford to do that, not even for the church."

"I am sorry to hear that, Master Roberts. Your journey was wasted."

"Yes, but I was glad to move around in a strange place and gather news."

"Did you hear any news of interest?"

"Mostly about the price of corn, or of white bulls." Master Roberts chuckled. "But some fellow did apprise me of an outrage which he had heard of in the North Country."

"What was that, pray?"

"It would seem that the Scotch King, King James, has been abducted."

"Abducted! A king!"

"Aye, this fellow told me that, led by a Lord Gowrie, the rebels seized the king and usurped the government of that country."

"Were you told why they did such a thing?"

"I am not clear on that. Seemingly they were trying to stop the French having influence at court and to stop their late Queen from returning."

"I doubt there is much chance of that, since our own Queen has her closely confined at Sheffield Castle."

"Those were my thoughts, also. If I were to wager, I would say that lady will not survive the axe much longer."

"Marry, she hath given our queen trouble enough to warrant it."

"Indeed. But it is a rare and foul thing to kidnap a king."

They rode on until they gained the border separating England from Wales, and halted briefly to wonder at the bank and ditch there which was said to have been erected by a Saxon king some eight hundred years previous to their time.

"A deal of work was expended on that, I'll wager," Tomos said. "I am told it runs all the way north to Prestatyn."

"Yes and all the way south to Casgwent."

They travelled onward for a few miles until the place where their roads parted. Master Roberts extended his hand to Tomos, who shook it heartily. "Well, sir, here we are. You must go your way and I must go mine. I wish you Godspeed."

"Likewise to you, Master Roberts. I am glad to have made your acquaintance."

Tomos and Maelwgyn turned onto the lonely, narrow road which few travelled save for they who had affairs in the tiny villages of Efancoed, Maestreylow, Llandewi-yn-Hwytyn and Pill Lledd, where stood the church of St. Mary and her holy well. This road led ultimately to Llanbister, and from there it would be another six long miles 'til home.

Maelgwyn found it hard, rough going, as much was uphill, and mud was deep on the road. In some places, the road was washed out, so they had to detour through fields. Both rider and mount were weary, anxious to be in their own place and were ravenous for sustenance.

About the only pleasant distraction for Tomos was when the road ran close to the River Lugg and there were ducks, coots and moorhens to be seen.

It was well dark as they passed through Llanbister. They went by the lovely little church of Saint Anno, where Tomos and Thomasina would be wed, and made for yet another lonely road that led to Pant-y-dwr and Sychnant Fawr.

It was with such laboring effort that Maelgwn plodded up the long, steep hill that, to spare him further uncomfort, Tomos dismounted and walked alongside him.

When, finally, they turned into the lane which led to Tomos' farm, both man and beast were fit for nothing but their beds.

XXXVI

It was almost noon when Tomos stirred and left his bed. He was still sore and much tired, but was exceeding glad to be at home.

He called his housekeeper, Gwenllian, and bade her prepare some ham from his own pigs, eggs from his own hens and ducks, bread from his own ovens, and ale from his own barrels in order to break his fast.

While Gwellian went about the business of getting his repast ready, Tomos pulled on his boots and surcoat and made a tour of the farm, ensuring first that Maelgwn was treated rightly, and then that all other stock were flourishing.

In this pleasant and satisfying pursuit, he was accompanied by his steward, Elwyn ap Rhys, a stout and steady fellow of some forty summers who had been in his employ ten years since. Elwyn gave him an account of events which had occurred on the farm, and in the locality, during Tomos' absence in Sussex.

Little of that account was of moment, except that the dun cow had expired, something not unexpected as she was of a great age, and that four new calves had been delivered of other cows. The corn was in good condition in the fields and would be ready for harvest in a few weeks, provided excess rainfall did not intervene. The root crops and cabbages planted in the upper field were as well as might be expected, the latter suffering only slightly from the caterpillars of the white butterfly.

Elwyn reported that the well was flush and working as it should, that repairs to the thatching on the main house were almost complete, and that the walls of the dairy had been recently washed and whitened.

"You have done well, Elwyn," said Tomos with a gratified sigh. "It seems I am hardly needed on my own farm for it to flourish."

"Indeed, I do have it under control, Master," said Elwyn, "but I should not want thee to stay away any longer."

"I have to go away again soon, but I am confident you will manage while I am gone. But more of that after I have broken my fast. Will you assemble all who work and live with me in the big barn, in one hour? I have much of importance to say to you. News I hope you will all welcome."

"Certainly, Master. It shall be as you instruct."

Sitting at the stout wooden trestle in his parlour, Tomos made short work of the thick slices of delicious Welsh ham and two each of his hens' and ducks' eggs. He wiped his platter with bread baked by Gwenllian the previous day, and emptied his tankard of ale. Then he strode over to the big barn, there to greet his employees and friends.

In addition to Gwenllian and Elwyn, there were Gwillym, the ploughman, Efan the carter, Gryffudd the dairyman and his maid, Angharad, Geraint the stockman, and Carys and Rhiannon the indoor maids.

As was only natural, Tomos addressed them in their own tongue. His words produced cries of pleasure and surprise when he told them he was to wed and that he would be going forth to fetch his bride from far away in England. He said they would take the special carriage from the sgubor fach, or little barn, which would be driven by Efan, carrying Carys, who would later attend as maid to

Thomasina. It would take them five days, possibly longer, he said, so they should come prepared with what clothing and supplies might be needed for such a journey.

He said that he himself would take two horses, Malgwn and Rhodri, a mighty, grey ambler, the one to ride, the other to run light behind the carriage to give relief to the other animal from time to time as needed.

Having received the assent of those who would be making the journey with him, he thanked them all for their kind attention, climbed down from the cask on which he had been standing to address them, and went to the stables. He went in to see Maelgwn and carefully tended that horse, checking to see that the steed would be fit to travel again so soon after his recent excursions.

After a night's rest and a bellyful of good feed, the animal seemed to be in exceeding good condition, so Tomos did stroke him and talk to him as was his wont.

Then, taking a bay cob from the stable, he saddled her and rode slowly, and happily, into Llananno to the clergyman's house to arrange for his wedding with Thomasina.

The Reverend Mr. Rosser was surprised to see Tomos, especially upon such an errand, but welcomed him in. He was an ancient gentleman, maybe of eighty summers or more, who was liked but little trusted by the local people because he had been an ardent Catholic when Queen Mary was on the throne, but had become a stalwart Protestant when the present Queen acceded. Having little right which his own possession of morality might bestow, he nonetheless liked to severely lecture others on their failings and frailties.

He questioned Tomos closely about Thomasina, and when he discovered her age, he did huff and clear his throat in displeasure. "Tomos Jones," he began in his high dry manner of speaking. "Can we be sure this is pleasing in the sight of God?"

"My wife will be well provided for should I predecease her. She will own the land, the farm and all the movables. Should she wish to be remarried, she would have the pick of the county for suitors. Can you deny this?"

"No, indeed—"

"And the woman comes to me of her own free will, and, what is more, she has agreed to learn the Welsh language, too."

"Well…"

The reverend gentleman cut short his objection when he saw Tomos open his pouch, produce a number of golden sovereigns and count them out, one by one, upon the table.

"Now I consider the matter, I am sure the Lord will look kindly upon your union," said Reverend Rosser.

"I thought you would better know the Lord's will and pleasure once you had reflected upon it," said Tomos.

"The wedding shall be in nine days' time then?" the old man asked.

"Possibly a day or two later, but that will not discommode you, sir?"

"Not at all. Duw a summer wedding! There's tidy! How splendid!" The old man smiled as he rubbed his hands together and regarded the money in front of him.

XXXVII

Everything was ready for the long journey in good time, and Tomos was much pleased by the alacrity with which those in his employ did make haste in the preparations. The sturdy carriage was repaired in every aspect, and repainted, and additional measures were added to increase the comfort of Carys, and later Thomasina, who were to ride therein.

Spare wheels made of good elm for the naves, oak for the spokes and ash for the fellowes were slung on the sides. Elwyn ap Rhys had even installed a spare oaken axle which he cunningly ran along the underside of the vehicle. This would add weight and might slow them down somewhat, he knew, but would be invaluable in the case of an accident on the hard and rocky roads they would encounter. He was aware that most villages had a blacksmith who could assist them in the event of mishap, but few were likely to have the raw materials at hand and wheelwrights were far between.

Both Maelgwn and Rhodri were well fed and shod and in exceeding fine condition, as were Sian and Blodwyn, those horses which would pull the carriage. Well secured were feed for the animals, and ample supplies of dry foodstuffs together with a barrel of ale to provide refreshment on the roads and to sustain them should they be unable to find lodgings.

Elwyn ap Rhys had affected a superb arrangement of all, and Tomos was in high praise of him and what he had accomplished.

The steward had been so diligent that they could leave a day earlier than was anticipated.

"Let us then not waste another minute," said Tomos impatiently. "Carys, Efan, get thy belongings. We shall not tarry further!"

The two mentioned did scurry away to the house and stables, quickly returning, each carrying a small bindle. They sprang lightly into the carriage and at Tomos's command, Efan cracked his whip. Blodwyn and Sian walked stately out of the farm gate, the carriage creaking behind them, and Rhodri tethered to the carriage brought up the rear.

Tomos made his grateful goodbyes to Elwyn and Gwenllian, waved his hat in the air, and, astride Maelgwn followed the carriage down the long hill.

Tomos was in rare spirits. The day was fine, if a trifle cool, but the winds were low. Underfoot the roads would be dry and firm. With God's grace, he hoped, they might reach, if not Hereford then maybe Monnington by nightfall. He felt fit and healthy, his brain was content, and his heart was bursting. He was going to bring his bride home.

38

As predicted, it was a long day, made longer than necessary by Tom getting lost after taking the wrong road at Presteigne. It led them to Droitwich, which was some miles out of their way to the north, but he got back on to the right track by finding the M5 South at Wychbold.

His original intention was to join the M4 East outside Bristol but when Tasin saw signs for The Cotswolds, she insisted he take a route through that beautiful area which has been attracting visitors for over a hundred years. So he left the motorway at Brockworth and took the A417, passing Birdlip, Elkstone, Winstone, Dunisbourne Abbots Dunistone Leer, Dunistone Rouse, Cerney Wick and Cricklade.

Sean, who had spoken to neither Tom nor Tamsin since the day's journey began, sat in the back seat, muttering to himself. "The sun has supreme dignity and we represent him by a circle having a visible centre," he said as if reciting a poem.

Tamsin and Tom ignored him but gave each other a nervous glance.

Tamsin adored the Cotswolds. She fell in love with its pretty villages of warm grey stone, which showed yellow when it was newly cut, and the many thatched roofs. She begged Tom to drive off in search of some of the places whose names she saw on signs.

He agreed, but said they could only make one detour because of time limitations, so he left the main highway past Elkstone, then wound along the narrow—sometimes single-track—lanes through Rapsgate, Woodmancote, North Cerney and Perrot's Brook before rejoining the highway at Baunton.

"The self same sun 'tis yet more, yet must wound, still with new knives of the same kind and ground," Sean said sonorously to himself as the car took a sharp turning.

They went on to the M4 East just past Swindon and stayed on it until Hungerford, when they veered south. Still fascinated by the quaint place names, Tamsin reeled them off as she saw the road signs: Speen, Tufton, Sutton Scotney, Ampney Crucis, Kings Worthy, Abbots Worthy, Hinton Apner, West Meon Hut, and Trotten.

At Winchester they turned to the east and finally came to the Downs.

"Neither the circle nor the line without the point can be artificially produced," Sean murmured as if in a trance.

Tom rolled his eyes and shook his head, sorrowfully. Tamsin fidgeted anxiously.

It was past five o'clock when Tom manoeuvred his way to Bepton and Cocking, and found the little village of Dropsorrow. Here he stopped the car and stretched.

They had been on the road for more than six hours, during which time Tom was concentrating on the driving while Tamsin had commanded the conversation, most of it about the places they passed through or near. At no time on the journey did Sean say anything to Tom or Tamsin; only to himself, mostly in an incoherent way.

"Well this is it," said Tom. "It must be around here somewhere."

Sean suddenly came alive and grabbed the map. "The lane to the manor should be coming up on our left at any time soon. Unless we passed it. Did either of you see a lane or a sign in the last few miles?"

"There were several on the right, but none on the left," Tamsin said.

"Then we should be alright," said Sean. "The art of navigation demonstrates how, by the shortest way, and in the shortest time, a sufficient ship between any two places assigned, may be conducted."

"Whatever," mumbled Tom. "We are way off the beaten track. I hope this place has running water and electricity."

They had to pull into a field gateway to allow a van to pass. Then they drove on, peering this way and that.

"There it is!" Tamsin cried. "Back there. That must have been it."

Tom stopped and reversed until they were level with a tiny lane, with grass growing in the centre, heading up hill into some trees. There at the side was a small sign saying 'Wistan Manor'.

"What do you think, Sean?" Tom asked.

"Yes!" Sean shouted. "This is it! I know it!"

"Alright. Here we go."

The lane emerged through a cluster of oaks onto the gravelled forecourt of the manor house. On one side there was a large, well-tended lawn, some attractive flower beds and the remnants of an orchard. The building was a strange one, being an amalgam of different styles and periods, the earliest appearing to be sixteenth century, which was well-represented by black and white half-timbering.

Tom brought the car to a scrunching halt in front of the huge, wooden door. They all peered out.

"What a great place," exclaimed Tamsin.

"This is it," said Sean. "What an incredible place. This is where he lived."

"You sure? How can you know?"

"Feel it, Tamsin. Feel it. Can you feel it? This is the place Dr. Dee leased after the Mortlake fire. Tom, can you feel it?"

"Er...I guess it could be the same place."

"Aye thankee God who is our only guide. All is enough, no more than at this tide," Sean cried, jumping out of the car and striding off into the grounds.

Tamsin and Tom unloaded their belongings from the trunk, and carried them into what passed for a lobby. It was little more than a hallway with a small table bearing a guestbook and a tiny bell. It was dark and their footsteps echoed on the ancient polished wood floors.

"It's like something out of a Stephen King movie," whispered Tamsin.

"I know. All we need now is a dark and stormy night with lightning and guttering candles."

"And vampires."

"May I help you?" The voice came from behind them and almost made them jump. It was a quiet voice, a smooth voice, an oily, vaguely unpleasant, voice.

They turned and saw a tall man somewhere between youth and middle age, slightly stooped and dressed in black.

"Oh, good evening," said Tom. "We did make reservations. It's one single room and one double."

"Ah, yes," said the man, looking in the book. "Mr. Dorch and Mr. Johnson isn't it?"

"Yes. The single room is for Mr. Dorch."

"I am Mr. Kelly, the manager. If you'll follow me, I will show you to your rooms. But where is Mr. Dorch?"

"He'll be in soon. He's looking around the grounds."

"I see. It's this way. I'm afraid we have no elevator, so we have go up two flights of stairs."

They followed the man—who did not offer to help with their bags—up the winding staircase until they were on the third floor. There were thick, but faded and worn, carpets on the floor, and the walls were covered with a long-out-of-date heavy, brown flock wallpaper.

The doors to the rooms were painted shiny black and bore the names of what they subsequently learned were South Saxon kings. Tom and Tamsin were given Aelthelbehrt while Sean's luggage was taken to Ealdwulf.

"May we have dinner tonight please?" Tamsin asked Mr. Kelly.

"Certainly, if you don't take too long. We stop serving at eight."

"Thank you. And breakfast?"

"Breakfast is from seven until nine-thirty."

A noise alerted Mr. Kelly to a new arrival. "And this must be Mr. Dorch coming."

"Good day," said Sean, out of breath from the climb.

"Ah, I see you are *that* Mr. Dorch. I recognize you from your motion pictures."

"It is gratifying to receive recognition," Sean said. "I thank thee."

"Well," said Kelly, giving Sean a strange look, "I shall leave you now. The dining room is on the ground floor, through the hallway and to the left. Remember, you must be there before eight."

Kelly left as silently as he had arrived and disappeared into the recesses of the great house.

XXXIX

Contrary to Tomos' fears that a well-stocked carriage, four horses and a young woman might prove tempting prey to villains, they were not accosted by any but friendly people in their journey through the Royal Forest of Dean.

Although the early mornings and the nights were a little colder than heretofore, the weather was surprisingly obliging. The parts of the forest where the canopy was open allowed the sun's warmth to reach them unchecked. But, though cooler, even more delightful were those stretches of road where the sunlight only came through as shafts of light and dappled shadows.

To his great amazement, Tomos had a reunion with the illustrious acquaintance from his journey in the other direction several days since. He was even more surprised that the Earl of Pembroke, the Queen's Warden, remembered him and his personal details.

"Good morrow, my lord."

"Good morrow, Tomos Jones of Bwlch y Sarnau!" said that important personage. "Am I pronouncing the place correctly?"

"Your Lordship makes a much better fist of it than most Englishmen do."

"Hah! Well, that is something. The Welsh tongue has so many traps for the English. It is a twisting, turning language which we find almost impossible to say and understand."

"Your Lordship has the knack, which most do not. I am sure that, were your Lordship to spend some time among the Welsh, you would be speaking like a native within a few years."

"That is kind of you to say so, Master Jones, but alas I have not the opportunity to do as you suggest, except occasionally in the western fringes of the forest. I know some Welsh people at Whitchurch, but am not required to spend more than a day a month there."

"Your Lordship has many important responsibilities."

"Indeed I do. But, pray, why do I see you going where you have shortly been? What takes you back to the south, and that so soon?"

"I am going to be reunited with my bride to be," Tomos said, and, indicating Effan and Carys, "These are my servants from the farm."

"Good and trusty they look, and no doubt are. But I must be on my way. God speed you to your bride, Tomos Jones!"

"I do humbly thank your Lordship. May God go with you."

The journey to Coberly was uneventful if tiring and, as night was falling, they were heartily glad to see the Seven Springs Inn ahead, and even gladder to know that the good mistress of that establishment had made provision for them.

XL

Richmond Palace was a magnificent edifice towering on the bank of the river Thames, at some remove from London. It was one of the Queen's favourites, second only to Placentia, and there she spent much time on the business of the nation, and on her own amusement. There she hunted stags in her Great Park and held court together with her nobles.

The palace had been builded by her grandfather, King Henry, the seventh of that name, and was so favoured by him that he left this world from that place in the year of Our Lord 1509. The place had been constructed in such a fashion as to be less cold than other palaces, so the Queen chose to spend a greater part of her winters there.

Since the palace could accommodate a goodly number of persons, Her Majesty was able to summon many musicians to her presence, there to indulge her in her greatest pleasures. The Queen did adore music and positively delighted in the dancing, believing it to be a wondrous form of exercise for all ages, and did frequently exhibit herself on the floor.

Her Majesty was an accomplished player upon the lute and virginals and did construct her own musical compositions, which were said to be tolerably good. She expected her court to be similarly interested in, and proficient at, the playing and the dancing and, while perforce all tried their utmost to please her, few were judged as expert as herself.

It was said that the Queen had over sixty musicians in her employ who were able to make the best of sackbuts, krumhorns, flutes, violas, cornets, recorders, lutes, and the using of their voices in song. In addition to these, she delighted to entertain the best players and composers in the land. Among those notables, Masters Byrd, Taverner, Morley, Tallis and Gibbons were frequent guests.

One of these composers was a very young man, no more than nineteen summers, one John Dowland, of whose songs the Queen was especially fond. She would bid him sing one of them, *My Tears Shall Flow*, time after time, even though he did protest that the work was unfinished and needed more effort spent upon it. Master Dowland accompanied himself upon the lute.

> *My tears shall flow from your springs,*
> *Ever exiled then let me mourn;*
> *Where the night's bird her sad infamy sings,*
> *There I shall live forlorn.*

"Ah, young sir," quoth the Queen, "with such talents, I do prophesy that you will have much greater success as you grow older."

"I humbly thank your Majesty," said young Dowland, bowing deeply and withdrawing into the ranks of personages.

"What shall we have now, Burghley?" the Queen asked her Lord Treasurer. "Shall it be a madrigal?"

"Your Majesty may have whatever pleases her."

"Then a madrigal it—"

The Queen was interrupted by the sudden and noisome entrance of Sir Francis Walsingham, accompanied by an armed guard of some half-dozen soldiers.

The Queen's outrage was at once apparent. "Walsingham, what means this rude intrusion? How dare you bring men at arms into my private quarters!"

"I beg your forgiveness," said Sir Francis, bowing very low indeed, "but these men are necessary to prevent harm to Your Majesty's royal person—"

At this the Queen blanked and there was a great gasp of surprise and dismay from the assembled company.

"—and to bring to justice a vile, contemptible and pernicious traitor!"

A loud babel of alarm and confusion seized the company, but the Queen silenced them, barking for order.

"Explain yourself, Sir Francis. For if you cannot, I promise it will be the worse for you!"

"Majesty," said Sir Francis drawing closer, "some months since, a letter came into my possession indicating that a plot was afoot to take Your Majesty's life. At that time, we knew not the sender nor the receiver of this missive, save that one of them was here at court."

"At court! Knew you of this, Burghley?" The Queen turned to her treasurer.

"Aye, I did, Madame. Sir Francis made me privy to the matter from the very start. We wished not to alarm Your Majesty, lest it come to nothing, or we should have informed you then."

"You took a mighty liberty, both of you! If this does not turn out well, by God, I shall give you cause to regret it!"

"For months our agents scoured the realm and the continent," said Sir Francis, "to find intelligence of this wretch and his foreign accomplices, and today we have our answers."

"Name these foreigners, Walsingham."

"It will come as no surprise to you, Madame, that Phillip, the King of Spain, is behind this villainy and has been putting in place the preparations for an armada to invade this country."

The crowd gasped in amazement and did break out into indignant cries and curses, each looking at the other and wondering who the domestic plotter might be.

Again the Queen called for silence.

"And tell me, Sir Francis, who be the traitor? Do you have his name?"

"I do, Your Majesty. His name is Sir Edward Luvington. Guards, seize and bind him at once!"

The guards at once proceeded to the far side of the room, where the terrified Sir Edward could be seen cowering against a wall. One of them felled him with a blow of his pike and the other bound him and dragged him from the chamber.

"Let him be sent for trial at once," the Queen pronounced. "If he be guilty, as you say he is, Walsingham, let us have his head as soon as may be meet. Now then, all save Sir Francis and my Lord Burghley may leave us at once."

The chamber emptied quickly, amid the cacophony of chatter, the slamming of doors, and musical instruments being humped along the floor.

When all were gone, the Queen turned to her counsellors. "Well, despite your presumption, it seems you have served us well in this matter. We thank you both."

"I am duty bound to inform Your Majesty," said Sir Francis, "that our success in unmasking the traitor was in no small part due to the efforts of Master John Dee."

"Ah, John Dee, you say? Well, well. Burhgley, see that all outstanding oweings and pledges to Dr. Dee be honoured without delay. May God bring good blessings to Dr. Dee and smile upon him and all his household."

212

XLI

Tomos and his party broke their fast very early, before light, and were on the road afore the hour of five. Carys was some peevish at having to rise so early, but soon regained her usual sunny disposition, and was laughing and singing as they went along. Efan, who said little in any event, tended to all four horses very diligently and gruffly bade his master good day.

It was important that they set off early, for they aimed for Marlborough that day, and it was a goodly distance off, some forty miles or more. The animals were in better spirits than the people, and they went forth at a good pace.

They passed through the Cotswold Hills, Tomos remembering how fond of these villages he was when first he saw them. He was happy to remake his acquaintance at Cockleford with the kind blacksmith who has reshoed Maelgwn. The fellow hailed them and asked Tomos to take a tankard of cider; but he had not the time, and with much thanks did press on.

Later in the day, as they were approaching Blunsden St. Andrew, they saw a number of men strung out along the road, and into the field, some of them peering through strange tubes atop three legs of wood. Others were holding tall staffs aloft and calling out uncommon names.

Curious indeed, Tomos halted Maelgwn, dismounted and walked over to the gentleman who appeared to be in charge of the operation.

"Good den," said he. "I am Tomos Jones from Wales. Marry, but I have not seen the like of this afore and beg to inquire what it is you are about, sir?"

"Good den, sir" said the gentleman. "My name is John Speed and these are my associates, Master Christopher Saxon and Master John Rudd."

The other two men suspended their activities and came over to them. They exchanged their greetings.

"Master Jones, we are map making."

"Map making? Indeed?"

"Verily. Her Majesty has charged us with mapping England and this is but one part of a massive exercise. We are traversing the entire realm in this endeavor."

"I am astonished," said Tomos, "but heartily glad I encountered you today. I know nothing of maps, nor indeed how they be made."

"I some years' time, when we are finished, I hope you will see the maps and think of this happy meeting," said Master Rudd.

"I shall. It was my privilege to have met you all."

They all shook hands and did return to their previous activities.

"Beth yw map, syr?" asked Efan as they got under way.

"Go brin fy mod yn adnabod fy hun ond mae'n ddogfen i arwain teithwyr," Tomos replied.

The good fellow had never heard of a map. Tomos was barely able to explain it to him, but did his best to say that it was some kind of guide for travellers, and that the men they had met were famous persons who enjoyed the Queen's confidence.

It was after dark when they reached Malborough and were unable to find lodgings, so they set up a makeshift camp. They did feed and water the horses in the River Kennett, light a fire, and hand around some bread and cheese, and then went to sleep under the stars.

XLII

Dr. Dee was busy at his desk with some mathematical calculations. He had long been of the opinion that there were many arts which beautified the mind of man, but of all of them none did more than those arts which are called mathematics. Further, he believed that one could not attain perfect knowledge of the subject without first being instructed in the principles of the elements of geometry. To this end, he had devised a number of charts to assist him in his studies. These he had affixed to the walls and, from time to time, he would twist in his chair to consult them.

This he was now doing, and was greatly vexed when he heard a knock at his door.

"Come!" Said he, tersely, for he hated to be interrupted when he was at some critical juncture in his deliberations.

"Excuse me, Master," said Talbot, obsequiously putting his head around the door.

"What is it?" demanded the doctor. "Do you not know that I am much engaged?"

"That's what I told her, but she insisted."

"What are you talking about, man?"

"'Tis the wench, Thomasina, she begs audience with the master."

Dr. Dee threw his pen upon the desk in frustration, and gathered his gown about him. "Very well. I will see her. But you should have waited until you were aware I was at liberty. This is the second time you have failed me, Talbot!"

"I am truly sorry, Master. Shall I show her in?"

"Yes, do so, but, Talbot…"

"Yes, Master?"

"See you close the door after her."

"Yes, Master."

Thomasina, evidently in some distress, entered and approach the doctor's desk. In a high sulk, Talbot made a show of slamming the door, but kept the handle fully turned, so that when the door closed he was able to silently reopen it sufficient to overhear what was said in the room.

"Thomasina, what is it? I am very busy."

"Forgive me, sir, but I was wondering if you had received any word of Master Tomos' progress into Wales."

"No, Thomasina, I have not. In faith, I did not expect to hear anything until he returned, as I do not suppose it would be convenient sending messages when on the move."

"Master, I would take it very kindly if you could send word to him to ask if the marriage could be held soon."

"Well, he told me it would take him five days and nights to achieve his farm in Radnorshire, a few days there to make preparations, and then a further five or six to repair to Dropsorrow."

"I see. I am sorry. I was anxious for him, but I do understand the length of time that be necessary to get to Wales and back."

"Is that it? Will there be anything further?"

"Well…I think…"

"What is it? Out with it, girl!"

"I best not say, sir. Faith, I best not."

"Ah!" said the doctor, carefully scrutinizing her. "I am able to discern some matters others cannot see. You are with child, are you not?"

"Yes, Master. I am."

"My cousin's child?"

"Yes, oh yes, of course, Master! Be most assured of that!"

"Very well. I shall send word to Bwlch y Sarnau and urge Tomos to make haste. I know my cousin loves you, Thomasina, so I do not think he will delay his departure more than is absolutely necessary."

"Thank 'ee, sir. I do thank 'ee from the bottom of my heart!"

"Very well. You may now go about your duties."

Thomasina curtsied and made for the door. Before she had reached it, Talbot quietly closed it fully, and ducked in behind the heavy drapes which separated the house from the sleeping quarters. From his hiding place, he heard her scurry down the passage to the kitchen.

Great was his triumph, his exaltation. "Now I have you!" he whispered. "Now I shall have both of you! You may think you can humiliate Edward Talbot with impunity, but I shall show you that you cannot. All who have treated me with indignity shall suffer. They will pay a heavy price, indeed!"

As soon as he was sure the passage was clear, Talbot did sneak out of the house and in the highest of spirits did hare down the lane towards West Dropsorrow village.

~

In a filthy corner of the village tavern, Ned Pascoe, John Nutall and George Plunkett were quaffing ale immoderately. Nutall was relating to the other two more misfortunes which had occurred on his uncle's farm.

"And when Amos the carter did bring out the big shire horse for the cutting—you know the one, Elspeth is her name, as peaceful as a lamb—she did suddenly lay down upon him and break his legs."

"No?!"

"Aye, one of them legs has been sawn off, and it bodes ill for t'other one. They say the gangrene will get it, too."

"Marry, that is bad news," Pascoe pronounced.

"Especially for the carter!" said Plunkett sagely.

"And that is not all," Nutall continued. "My auntie were apicking early apples for the cooking—you knows they is right sharp when they is little, which is what she is wanting for her chutney—when she see something in the grass."

"What were it, John Nutall?" Plunkett enquired.

"You woan believe it, but it were a snake with a bird in its mouth."

"Well, I never!" Pasco declared.

"And her says that the bird was still singing!"

"Wondrous, indeed!" Plunkett said, taking a hearty pull on his ale. "With such strange goings on, you may think God and the saints had deserted us."

"I heard tell there be more crop failures over Graffham way," said Nutall.

"And, no doubt, we will get rain day after day come t'harvest," Plunkett said.

"These is bad times aplenty, for sure," Pascoe opined into his tankard.

Just then a shaft of daylight indicated that the door had opened and someone had entered the premises. They looked up and saw Ned Talbot from the big house making his way towards their table.

"Good morrow, Master Talbot."

"I wish I could say 'good morrow', but it is not," Talbot said, his voice filled with dread. "I have news which will wither the marrow in thy bones."

"In God's name, speak!" Plunkett urged.

"I have got this from the very source, from their own lips."

"What? What?"

"The red-headed wench is with child and the doctor, my master, is its father!"

"No!!"

"Aye, 'tis so. I heard it from their own mouths."

"By heavens! So the maid and the sorcerer have conceived a child together!" Plunkett could scarcely credit the news.

"The progeny of a magician and a witch. God help us all," said Pascoe.

"I needs not tell thee what fiendish things may come about if the creature is born?"

"May God preserve us if such a thing should come to pass," said John Nutall. "Thank 'ee for telling us this, Master Talbot. I think we all know what must be done."

"Since I am employed by the sorcerer, my part in this must be secretive and discreet to we four alone," Talbot admonished his companions.

"Fear not, Master Talbot. Your part in this is safe with us. Get thee gone now, sir, and leave all to us."

"Aye," said Pascoe. "We will arouse the village."

"Indeed we shall," said Plunkett grimly. "It is high time there was a reckoning for all the ill which us has been visited with of late."

As Talbot quietly slipped out of the tavern, the three men were already moving from table to table, spreading their poison.

XLIII

The morning was cold and wet. The wind was ablowing exceeding strong. The horses were restless and bretty. Everyone was in a foul mood as the weather made it impossible to properly dry off or to have anything hot to eat or drink.

Tomos and his party set off for Basingstoke a sorry, bedraggled and dispirited crew. Nobody said a word. Carys made no singing or laughing today. The only sounds were the creaking of the carriage, the jingling of the harnesses and the snorting of the animals.

To add to their discomfort, near Kingsclere they hit a large rock protruding from the road and broke a wheel. 'Twas lucky they had a spare, but much time was taken lifting and propping up the carriage to fit the new wheel. Even the normally quiet Efan was given to such cursing and swearing that Tomos had to reprimand him that this manner of language in front of Carys was not proper.

When the repairs had been effected they struggled onwards, wet, hungry and miserable. The rains did increase and the winds did whip around their faces and lash at their clothing.

After an eternity of enduring these adverse conditions, they approached Wooton St. Lawrence on the outskirts of Basingstoke, and saw a rider making haste towards them. The poor fellow was exhausted and sodden from the rain. His horse was much fatigued and was lathered and panting.

"Master Jones. It that you, is it not?" asked the rider.

"That is I. Do I not know you?"

"You do, sir. I am a servant of your cousin, Dr. John Dee."

"You look all in, sir. Pray dismount. What is your mission?"

"I bring you this letter from my master," said the fellow, reaching into his jerkin for the missive and handing it to Tomos.

Tomos huddled down against the carriage to shelter from the wind, and did open the letter. This is what he saw:

> Cousin. I bid you come with all haste. Thomasina is with child. Come at once.
>
> John Dee

Tomos jumped up, stuffed the letter into his waist and turned to the rider. "You, my friend, stay here with my people and spend the night with them." And to his servants did say, "I have to go immediate as I can. I shall take Maelgwn, with Rhodri in tow. When the one is tired from bearing me, I shall mount the other."

"Ydy Meistr." Carys and Efan spoke in unison.

"You best know the way," Tomos said to Dr. Dee's servant. "You make sure Efan does not get lost."

"I will."

"Then I shall ride without rest or stop until I reach my cousin's door. Farewell! Ffarwel. Pob lwc!"

Tomos mounted Maegwn, attached a rope from his saddle to Rhodri's bridle, and thundered off into the blackness of the night.

XLIV

Villagers were huddled in small groups along the main street and around the market cross of Dropsorrow. Jon Nuthall, Ned Pascoe, and George Plunkett were moving from group to group, spreading word of Thomasina's pregnancy and invoking in inflaming terms the things which could occur were her baby to be born.

In one of these groups, the Reverend Mr. Grahame made a show of calling for moderation and reticence, but that gentleman was sorely pressed on all sides to show a manner of leadership that did not naturally come to him, and that he did not wish to assume.

"Reverend, we expect you to lead us in stamping out this evil," said Plunkett in a threatening way." And if you do not, us will be thinking you be slipping back into the ways of Queen Mary's Catholics."

"That is outrageous," responded the vicar. "There be no connection between the two. I am a more upright Protestant than you, George Plunkett, and all I am saying is let us be temperate in our behaviour. Violence begets violence, we told in Matthew 26, verse 52. Yet again, Psalm 37, verse 8 doth say 'Refrain from anger, and forsake wrath! Fret not yourself; it tends only to evil'!"

"Aye, but Matthew 11:12 doth say: And from the days of John the Baptist until now the Kingdom of Heaven suffereth violence and the violent shall take it by force!" rejoined Plunkett.

"It cannot be right for good men to stand by and allow evil to flourish!" quoth Mistress Adams, the baker's wife.

"Aye, thou knows what evils have befallen us of late, vicar," said Jon Nutall. "The failing of crops, the birthing of unnatural things, the strange omens all around us."

"Aye!" the villagers did shout as one.

"If thou do not lead us, we shall not be led by thee when all is over," Ned Pascoe said, his voice dark with menace. "If we are let down by thee in this most grievous matter, 'ee cannot expect us to meekly troop into thy church week after week, giving offerings of our hard-earned money, of which we have but little."

The vicar had his back to the wall of a house next to the blacksmith's forge, and he was aware that the hulking form of Kit Browne, the smith, hammer in hand, was fast encroaching upon him. He was sorely troubled and knew not what to do for the best, but he reasoned that neither his injury nor death could be providential, and that regardless of any entreaties he might make, the villagers were bound to do their own bidding. Therefore, he allowed that, in the longer term, it would be better for the church were he to take the lead, rather than to be a straggler behind the mob.

"Please do not misunderstand me, good people. I say only that we should not get so out of control as to harm one another in any scuffling or skirmishing."

"He has a point there," said Kit Browne. "Us don't want ourselves to be hurt. So, for God's sake, I say, let us keep pikes and swords aloft and not at our sides where they can injure ourselves or each other."

The crowd murmured their assent at this wise counsel and did raise their weapons and staffs above their heads.

The Reverend Grahame straightened his cassock, pulled his gown about him and did raise high his bible. His stentorian voice was easily heard above the hubbub. "Forward, good people! In the name of our Lord Christ, let us go onward like an army of God! To the big house! Let us seize the witch!"

A great hurrah did go up from the mob as they followed Mr. Grahame and in a great procession, slowly moved up the street in the direction of the manor house.

The light was starting to fade as they wound up the lane to Dr. Dee's house, the reverend in the lead and Pascoe, Nuthall and Plunkett urging the crowd to make haste and not to straggle. They surged into the forecourt and gathered noisily on the gravel by the front door. On Nuthall's instructions, a party of men were dispatched from the crowd and headed for the rear of the house.

Mr. Grahame and Pascoe went up the stone steps and did pound upon the big oaken door, Pascoe with the stock of his pike, Mr. Grahame with his silver-knobbed cane. All this was watched, with great delight, by Talbot from an upper window.

"Come forth, Master Dee," called the vicar. "Come forth. We have serious business with thee and will not be denied!"

The mob did echo his words, crying, "Come forth! Come forth!"

Whereupon the door did creak open, revealing the doctor, dressed from head to foot in deepest black.

"What does this unruly rabble require of me that they should so disturb my peace in such an outlandish fashion?"

"We demand that you produce the witch!" cried Pascoe.

"Witch? There is no witch here, you blockhead," said Dr. Dee with great spirit. "If you had the sense you were born with, you would be gone back to your homes. Doth hear me, sirrah?"

"Nay, Doctor Dee," said Pascoe. "Thomasina is a witch. The whore carries a hellhound in her belly!"

"You are indeed an ignorant rabble!" cried the doctor. "You know nothing of which you speak. The girl is innocent. A more good, honest, hardworking, and faithful servant never lived!"

At this the mob was berserk, howling and screaming.

"Aye, faithful to the devil," shouted one.

"She bent her back for you, sorcerer," cried another.

"Worshipper of Satan," did yell a third.

'Hear this, you lawless mob," Dr. Dee said severely, "and you too, Mr. Grahame, who should know better: this woman is a servant under my roof and in that capacity commands my protection. You shall not have her. I utterly deny your request!"

"You had best comply, doctor," said Mr. Grahame, "or I will not answer for the consequences and the deeds of these good people. They be sorely pressed and would be satisfied."

"I do not surrender to fools or blackguards. Or to those whose feeble minds have been addled by superstition. I say again, you shall not have her!"

At this moment there was a commotion from the side of the house, where those who had earlier been dispatched to the rear now reappeared, dragging a struggling Thomasina between them.

"We have the witch! We have her!"

The mob became wild with joy, some dancing, some jumping up and down, and all cheering mightily.

"We caught her trying to escape over the back pasture. Her was heading for the downs when us trapped her, like a vixen on the run!"

While Mr. Grahame, Pascoe and Kit Browne did restrain Dr. Dee, the latter by punching him hard in the face, the mob descended upon Thomasina and, lifting her up, did bear her aroint, and did turn back towards the village.

From his position on the ground, Dr. Dee hauled himself on to his elbow and did watch them go, pouring down the lane. He tried to stand, but was unable and, falling back, did become unconscious.

A scarce two miles aroint, urging Rhodri into a lathering gallop, Tomos Jones came thundering down the road, a panting Maelgwn running behind him. On the crest of the hill, he pulled up and gazed on the sight before him. In the distance he saw the mob nearing the village, but, not understanding it, he spurred the horse on towards the manor house.

Tomos cantered into the forecourt and, seeing his cousin on the ground, abruptly reined in his mount, slid from the saddle and rushed forward. He quickly kneeled down and, raising the doctor's head, strained to hear the words the injured man was trying to utter.

"Speak, cousin," said Tomos in high distress. "What has occurred? Who has done this to you?"

"Go to the village!" Dr. Dee said in a hoarse, laboured whisper. "They have Thomasina."

"They have Thomasina? What do you mean, cousin?"

"They have taken her for a witch! Go!"

A look of horror came to Tomos' visage as he leapt to his feet. "God's death! Get up behind me quickly!"

Speedily he mounted, pulling Dee up with him, and hurtled down the lane towards the village.

At the market cross, a group of villagers were putting the last touches to a stack of hay bales, brush, sticks and branches as the rest of the mob streamed down the street, driving Thomasina before them with pikes and staffs with which they were beating and sticking her. They were spitting at her and crying 'witch', 'whore' and 'devil's harlot'.

Her arms bound to her sides, they lifted Thomasina bodily into the centre of the stack of combustibles, where two ill fellows then tied her to the cross. The crowd cheered loudly. Shouts of 'burn the witch!' rang out through the rapidly falling darkness.

A great howl of joy arose from the mob as Ned Pascoe applied a flaming brand to the hay. In pious tones, Mr. Grahame invoked Divine authority for the purification of Thomasina's soul.

The howling became deafening as the flames flickered upwards, and as they passed around her legs and licked about her body, she did utter a long, bloodcurdling scream of agony and torment. In such a fashion did the beautiful, young Miss Thomasina depart this world.

Clattering into the village on the exhausted Rhodri, Tomos and Dr. Dee arrived just in time to see the flames reach Thomasina's beautiful, red hair, which instantly flared with added brightness and, for some seconds, did look like a diabolical, grotesque halo.

Realizing that they were too late, Tomos burst into uncontrollable tears, heavily sobbing on his horse's neck.

The fire now burned so brightly that no sign of Thomasina could any longer be seen. Cast by such a light, the shadows of the waving, cheering, dancing crowd maniacally flickered on the walls of the houses.

Reflecting the flames, Dr. Dee's haggard and scarred face was contorted with anguish.

45

Anxious not to miss the eight o clock deadline for dinner, Tamsin and Tom hurriedly unpacked their bags and cases, hung up their clothes and had a hurried wash. Then they went to Sean's room and knocked on the door.

"Sean, it's seven forty-five. We're going down to dinner. Are you coming?" Tom called.

There was silence from the other side. They knocked again, and just when they were about to leave, they heard a strange voice from within. It was Sean's voice, but was low and guttural.

"I cry you mercy, I crave your pardon, pray pardon. Leave me be. Thou knowest I have work to do."

"Knock it off, Sean, Stop messing around. If you don't go down soon, you'll get nothing to eat."

"That goose girl does not have no sense. His singing were more better than thine! The most smallest pig has the most biggest ears," came the reply.

"Don't be a horse's ass, Sean. Stop fucking around!"

"Please, Sean. Come down with us," Tamsin exhorted.

"Upon thine visage I see a coral blush so fine, as a rose before the bloom, seated daintly above thine chin and below such a divinely sculpted nose as e'en to turn an angel."

"This is a waste of time," said Tom.

"Sean, please come now," Tamsin pleaded.

"God's teeth, thou art a drudge withal."

"Good bye, Sean," said Tom. "I guess we shall see you at breakfast."

"Thou art a swollen and a festering nave, dim of wit and slow of tongue!"

"That's it!" Tom said angrily. "If he wants to play silly buggers, let's go without him."

They descended the loudly-creaking staircases, went down the dark passage and entered the dining room through a door of ancient oak which was almost too heavy to push open. Inside, the room was delightful, with windows overlooking the grounds, sparking white tablecloths and gleaming, heavy cutlery.

A smiling local woman offered them their pick of all the tables, since there were no other diners, and so they sat in one of the window bays. They were glad to find that the disturbing, uncomfortable Mr. Kelly was nowhere in evidence.

The food was surprisingly good, much better than they had expected. That they were both in a bad mood caused by Sean's behaviour did not prevent them from enjoying what was definitely the best meal they had eaten so far.

To start, they both had a delicious Potage St. Germain, bursting with fresh young peas and fresh mint, its rich bright green interrupted by a swirl of white cream. Then Tamsin had roasted grey-legged partridge with a wine sauce, game chips and asparagus. Tom ordered the pithivier, a delicate pie filled with chunks of venison, duck and woodcock in a rich gravy. With this, they positively salivated over a bottle of considerably under-priced 2010 Musigny Grand Cru.

Tamsin then had fresh strawberries and cream for dessert, while Tom tried the cheese plate, comprising Sussex Blue, Sussex Brie and Idle Hour, a semi hard cheese with creamy, citrus undertones.

"Is this a temporary phase?" asked Tamsin. "Or is it a stage in a natural and an irreversible progression?"

"If we could eat like this every day, I wouldn't care what it was."

"Idiot! I meant Sean's behaviour."

"Oh, sorry. It's hard to know when he's deliberately saying all these crazy things to get into character, and when it might be some mental aberration."

"I wish we could get some kind of professional help."

"Where and how? We'd have to get some psychiatrist to agree to pretend to meet him casually, so he wouldn't suspect. And we're in a strange country, miles from anywhere."

"No, of course we couldn't arrange that," said Tamsin ruefully. "I guess we'll just have to see how things play out."

"We don't have much choice," said Tom gloomily.

It was about two-thirty when Tamsin and Tom were awakened by a blood-curdling scream from the other side of the wall. They looked at each other for a moment, then there was another scream, louder than the first.

Tom leapt out of bed, hastily pulled on some clothes, then rushed next door and burst into the bedroom.

Sean was sitting up in bed, streaming with perspiration and eyes wide with fright.

"What is it, Sean? What's wrong?"

"Terrible things," Sean said in a hoarse and laboured manner. "Mine eyes have seen the most terrible sights."

"It was just a dream, Sean."

Just then, Tamsin, clutching her nightie around her, entered the room and stood by Tom.

Sean looked up, saw her, and stretched out his hand. "Oh, Tomos, forgive me. Please forgive me!" he pleaded in a quaking voice, then fell back on the pillow and passed out.

"What's going on?" demanded Kelly, entering in an old-fashioned, striped dressing gown. "What's the disturbance?"

"It's alright, Mr. Kelly," said Tamsin. "Mr. Dorch just had a nightmare, He'll be alright now. He's already asleep."

"Very well," said Kelly. "Some of us have to be up at six."

They watched him creak away down the corridor, pulled the bedclothes over Sean and returned to their room.

"Has he ever done that before?" asked Tamsin when they were snuggled back in bed.

"Done what?"

"Called you Thomas?"

"It didn't sound like 'Thomas'. It sounded more like 'Tomeoce'."

"Weird."

"Yes. And I have a feeling it's only going to get weirder."

46

When Tom awoke the next morning the bed was empty. Through the window, it looked like a fabulous day, with swallows swooping and diving, sparrows chirruping, and that most English of all summer sounds, the wood pigeon's coor-coor in the distance.

Tom hastily washed, shaved, pulled on his clothes and a sweater and went down the creaking staircases.

When he heaved open the heavy door and entered the dining room, he saw that Tamsin had already finished her breakfast and was just sipping a final coffee.

"You were up early," said Tom.

"I didn't want to wake you. You looked so peaceful, especially after the drama last night."

"Yeah. That was quite a performance!"

"It must have been some dreadful dream. Our friend Kelly seemed quite put out."

"He sees like a real creep."

"He is kind of weird."

"It looks like you've had your breakfast. What did you have?"

"I wallowed in the lap of luxury. I had the most expensive dish on the menu. A lobster omelette made with organic eggs, Scottish lobster, shallots, sour cream and tarragon. It cost £35.00!"

"Jesus!"

"It was absolutely delicious. You should try it."

"Maybe I will," said Tom. "Any sign of our Elizabethan lunatic today?"

"Tom!" Tamsin chided. "That's not nice! But no, not a sign as yet. I listened at his door but I could hear nothing."

"I guess he'll be down when he's ready. I sure hope he's more coherent than he was yesterday."

"Well, I'm going to leave you to deal with Sean."

"Why, what are you going to do?"

"It's such a lovely day, I thought I would walk into West Dropsorrow and have a look around."

"That's quite a way to walk."

"I'll be fine. There's no rain in the forecast, so it'll be a real treat."

"Okay. Enjoy."

"Why don't you and Sean come along later in the car? I'm going to poke about there most of the morning, taking pictures and stuff."

"Okay. Have a good time. See you later."

Tamsin leaned over and gave him a kiss, hitched up her shorts, slung her bag over her shoulder and left the dining room.

Shortly afterwards, the waitress came in and took his order. Not fancying seafood early in the morning, Tom did not order the same as Tamsin, but he did feel like pampering himself. So he decided to have the scrambled eggs en brioche with mushrooms and fried potatoes.

He was tucking into the delicious food when Sean staggered in. He was pale, unshaven, haggard and red-eyed. He slumped into the chair left vacant by Tamsin.

"Good morning, Sean. How are you feeling? You had a bad night. You made us worried."

"I feel like the depths of Hell," said Sean thickly. "What has occurred that you should worry?"

"Apparently, you had a bad dream. You were screaming and hollering. Must have been a real nightmare."

"Was it really a dream?"

"How do you mean?"

"Or was it real?"

Tom looked at him carefully, then poured him a cup of coffee. "Tell me, Sean, who's Tomeoce?"

"What?"

"You called me Tomeoce last night."

Sean stared out of the window, rubbing the back of his head. "Tomeoce....Tomeoce..."

"It must have been part of your dream," said Tom. "Anyway, drink your coffee. Why don't you have some eggs?"

"Eggs, butter, bread and small beer," muttered Sean strangely, as if reciting a childhood rhyme.

"I don't know about the beer, but if you really want it, I'm sure they can get it for you."

"Trouble not them, nor yet thyself."

"I thought we might go into the village later."

"Yes.... the village of West Dropsorrow."

"Yes, that's right. Tamsin has already left."

"Left?" Suddenly Sean was alert. "She has gone to the village? Tell me it is not so!"

"Sure. She left about half an hour ago. She said she was going on foot because it was such a lovely day."

"Nooooo!" Sean let out a long, low, tormented protest. "We must follow lest we be too late."

"Calm down, Sean. Finish your coffee. I'm going to have another cup."

"Oh, I greatly fear we may already have tarried o'er long."

Sean put his head in his hands and rocked from side to side. He sounded like he was crying softly to himself. Tom watched him, half in disbelief, and half in horror. A horror whose nature he could describe nor define.

47

Since the weather was so fine, Tom suggested they also walk to the village, but Sean made no response. When Tom took this as assent and set out, Sean stumbled silently along at his side.

It really was a spectacular day, hot and dry with little or no wind, and deep blue skies only slightly punctuated by tiny wispy clouds. Every breed of wild bird to be found in Sussex at that time of year seemed to be in furious competition to be heard, and the air was alive with their songs.

Tom's mood was upbeat. He had eaten a fine breakfast, was now completely sure he was in love with Tamsin, and planned to ask her to marry him at an early opportunity. In addition to being an amazingly beautiful woman, she was highly intelligent and had a well-developed sense of humour. They got along so well, very rarely disagreed, liked many of the same things, laughed a lot, and their love-making was beyond wonderful.

Sean's demeanour, on the other hand, was far from good. He slumped forward as he shambled along, muttering incoherently to himself. Tom thought there had been a very marked decline in Sean's condition since his dream—if dream it was—last night. Even though his behaviour was strange and uncommunicative in previous days, he now presented like a significantly different person entirely. He had not uttered any intelligible word since breakfast and seemed completely unaware of his surroundings.

They proceeded towards West Dropsorrow along lovely, narrow country lanes with hedges which were ablaze with honeysuckle, celandine, thistles, campion, dog violets, foxgloves, cow parsley, daisies, buttercups, dog roses, and loosestrife. Darting among the many blooms were a myriad of bees, bumble bees and butterflies. The sensation produced by these flowers—with their dazzling display of yellows, golds, purples, reds, whites, and blues—was enhanced by their scent lying heavily in the air.

In addition, hedge sparrows scuttled among the branches of the hedgerows, wagtails and wrens flitted from twig to twig, and finches chirruped among the leaves. Occasionally, a tiny shrew scurried in the ditches of the lanes, and a rabbit would shoot across in front of them. More than once, Tom noticed a slow-moving hedgehog nosing its way among the roots.

Tamsin, who had almost an hour's start on the others, had been all around the village, taking photographs with her phone, going into quaint little shops, and imagining what it would be like to live in some of the cozy, small-windowed cottages with their neat white-painted gates and front doors surrounded by trellised roses.

She had taken nearly all the pictures she wanted, except for a long shot of the street taken from the market cross. She had been prevented from taking this photograph by a large family of Japanese tourists which was occupying the steps and plinth, having a picnic lunch. The wind had risen somewhat in the last half hour and the family had trouble chasing their fluttering sandwich wrappings.

Eventually, the Japanese gathered up their litter, packed up their belongings and vacated the cross, just as Sean and Tom walked into the street. Tamsin climbed up to the top step of the plinth and aimed her phone. As she did so, the wind picked her long, gleaming red hair and tossed it about her head.

Seeing this, Sean started to run forward, his arms flying. "Noooooooooooooo!"

His cry attracted all others in the street, who turned to observe this strange figure advancing on the market cross.

"Stop!" he shouted, "She is innocent! She is innocent! Stop!"

He charged forward, knocking tourists and villagers out of his way, until he came to the foot of the cross, faltered, collapsed and, quivering and moaning, passed out.

"Better call an ambulance," said a voice in the crowd.

48

The ambulance took less than twenty minutes to arrive, during which time attempts by various people to revive Sean were unsuccessful. The attendants secured Sean to a stretcher, administered oxygen and put him in the vehicle.

Tom asked the driver where they were taking Sean and was told they would be going to the Midhurst Community Hospital in Easebourne, some five or six miles away.

"Tamsin, could you go with him in the ambulance while I go back and get the car? I'll meet you at the hospital."

"Why don't you go with him, and I'll get the car?" Tamsin sounded put out.

"You're not covered by the insurance. If you had an accident while driving it could cost us thousands."

"He's your friend." Her tone was strangely indignant.

"Please, Tamsin!"

"No, I'll come with you and we'll both go to the hospital as soon as we get the car."

"Alright, alright."

To the driver Tom said: "We have to get our car from Wistan Manor. We should be with you in an hour and a half."

"Okay, sir," replied the driver. "I'll them to expect a Mr...?"

"Johnson."

"Mr. Johnson. Right. What's the patient's name?"

"Sean Dorch."

"Not the actor chappie?"

"That's him."

"Well, I never! Okay, we're off."

The walk back to the manor was hurried and devoid of conversation. Tom knew that something other than Sean's collapse had occurred, but was not exactly sure what it was. He was secretly appalled by Tamsin's attitude at the ambulance, but could not explain it. He was not anxious to find out, so asked her no questions.

Eventually, they arrived at the manor, the way back seeming twice as long as the outward journey.

First looking at the map so he would know the way to Easebourne, Tom drove off, and in half an hour they were there, the hospital looking more like a suburban villa than a medical facility.

After they had waited for about twenty minutes, a doctor appeared.

"Are you with Mr. Dorch?"

"Yes, we are."

"I am Dr. Rajani. I have examined your friend and find that all his vital signs are okay. There is nothing wrong with him physically. I can only conclude he has experienced a serious mental episode."

"What does this mean?" Tamsin asked impatiently. "What has to be done now?"

"I am a general practitioner so I am not equipped to deal with something like this. We are sending him to the Department of Psychiatry at Eastbourne General."

"Aren't we already in Eastbourne?" Tom asked.

"No, this is Easebourne. It is very confusing, I know. Eastbourne is about 60 miles away. The doctors there will know what to do."

"When will you send him?" Tamsin asked.

"Right away. If you wish, you can follow the ambulance. I'll tell the driver to keep an eye out for you, so you don't get lost."

It took them over an hour and a half to get to Eastbourne, which turned out to be a large seaside resort bristling with boarding houses and hotels. The General was a very large hospital and, after parking, they almost got lost before finding the Department of Psychiatry.

Once there they waited more than an hour before a distinguished-looking man in a three-piece suit came out to them.

"Hello," he said, sounding very much like Hugh Grant, "allow me to introduce myself. I am Mister Hartley-Simpson."

"Aren't you a doctor?" Tom asked.

"Well, yes, but I'm a specialist, so they call me Mister. It must be very confusing for Americans."

"Canadians," Tamsin corrected.

"I do beg your pardon. I am so sorry."

"What about Mr. Dorch?" she said brusquely. "What's his condition?"

"He is fast asleep now and should sleep for several more hours. I am unable to predict with any precision what his condition will be when he awakens, but it is clear he has suffered a crisis of some sort which has resulted in his normal functions being overwhelmed. May I ask if he has been exposed to some experience which might predispose his condition?"

Mr. Hartley-Simpson listened very carefully, occasionally making notes, as Tom and Tamsin told him the entire account of Sean's drinking, of his preoccupation with his forthcoming role as Dr. Dee, of various episodes along the way, and of the recent events at Wistan Manor and in West Dropsorrow.

"Ah. That makes it quite clear now. Acute stress, an unhealthy obsession and abnormal consumption of alcohol all would render him susceptible to an extraordinary level of delusion."

"Yes, that's what has been happening," said Tom.

"He was muttering a great many things I could not fully comprehend," said Hartley-Simpson, "it sounded very much like Middle

English, although I am far from being an expert in philology."

"He's been repeating things that Dr. Dee said in the sixteenth century," said Tom.

"And he's been running about waving his arms," Tamsin added.

"Then I fear it may be much more serious than I thought," said Hartley-Simpson. "It seemed to me at first that your friend might be suffering from a combination of histrionic and narcissistic personality disorders. But now I think we can narrow it down to a form of grandiose delusional disorder."

"Are you familiar with this condition in your practice?" Tom inquired.

"Yes, to some extent, but it is not seen often. I am very much afraid that in these cases the patient may never recover."

"What?" Tamsin cried.

"Unfortunately, yes. There are some precedents for obsessive identification by an actor. The most celebrated case, which was diagnosed as manic depression and bipolarism, was Jeremy Huggins, who collapsed on a film set. His condition seems to have been compounded by the use of lithium, which is not the case here."

"Huggins?" Tom said, "I don't think I've heard of him."

"You know him as Jeremy Brett."

"Sherlock Holmes!" Tamsin exclaimed.

"Yes, indeed," said Hartley-Simpson. "He died in 1995 after a lengthy illness. Of course, I didn't attend that case, but I understand that he believed he actually was Sherlock Holmes. I have been told—whether it is true or not I can't say—that he used to run around the corridors of the hospital, shouting, 'Watson, the game's afoot!' A sad case. Something similar may have befallen your friend. Only time will tell."

"What now, doctor?"

"We'll keep him here for a week. If there is no change then we'll have to send him to a longer-term facility, probably Meadowfield in

Worthing."

"Thank you," said Tom. "We'll check back with you in a few days. My funds are running low so I'm not sure how long I can afford to stay in England."

"Ah. Does he have any family we could contact?"

"None that I know of."

"That is very unfortunate. Well, let's see how it goes."

In sober silence Tom and Tamsin drove back to Wistan Manor. Tom was turning over in his mind all Hartley-Simpson had said, and was wondering how he could face looking after Sean, and what would become of them both when he ran out of money.

As they were pulling into the forecourt of the Manor, Tamsin put her hand on Tom's arm and slid to the back of his neck. "Tom, honey, I've got something to tell you. I've made a decision. You're not going to like it."

"What is it?"

"I'm going to get my stuff and head out. This is all too weird for me. I've got to get away. You can see that, can't you, Tom?"

"No, I can't," Tom said, pushing her hand away. "You're just going to walk out on me? Just like that? What about Sean?"

"He's your friend, like I said. You're the best one to look after him. You don't need me."

"Yes, by God, I do!" Tom cried. "I do need you. I love you, Tamsin."

"Nah, you love firm young flesh. You're just hung up on young pussy. You'll get over it."

Tamsin hopped out of the car and headed for the Manor.

Tom bit his lip and pounded the dashboard with his fist, desperately trying not to cry. He was still sitting there ten minutes later when Tamsin emerged wearing her hiking boots, her knapsack slung around her shoulder.

"Maybe I'll track you down later in Halifax. To find out how

Sean's getting along. Thanks for everything, Tom."

Tom nodded dumbly. Tamsin bent into the car and gave him a gentle kiss on the cheek, then she strode away down the lane.

Tears were streaming down Tom's face as he watched her go.

49

After Tamsin had left, Tom dragged himself out of the car and sorrowfully climbed the stairs to his room. He could still detect her scent there, which increased his acute sense of loss. He dried his eyes and sat looking out of the window, asking himself what he had to do in light of Sean's condition.

He supposed that Kelly should be informed that Sean's room would no longer be required, that sooner rather than later the expensive rental car should be returned, and that Liz should be told.

And the realization came to him that Edgar Sollows should be informed that there was no way Sean could possibly fulfill his contract for the movie. Since he had no way to contact Sollows, or the Luvenstein person Sean had told him about, Tom thought he should call Sean's agent, Benny.

He didn't have a number, but knew the name of the agency in New York and, after some rigmarole, got it from directory assistance. He explained to the receptionist who he was and why he was calling. She sounded dubious, but when he told her that Sean was in hospital she agreed to put him through.

"Mr. Rosen, you don't know me, but I'm Tom Johnson and I am a friend of Sean Dorch. I'm calling from England. I thought I should tell you about him."

"I know who you are. You're calling me about Sean? What the hell is going on? I've been trying to get a hold of Sean for weeks. Where has he been?"

"He hasn't called you?"

"The hell he has! Sonofabtich hasn't checked in with me since you guys left."

"Right now he's in the hospital. And it's bad news. He's very sick and likely to stay that way for quite some time."

"Jesus! What's wrong with him?"

"It looks like a total mental breakdown. It means he won't be able to do the movie."

"What movie?"

"The Dr. Dee movie."

"There is no Dr. Dee movie, at least not yet."

"What do you mean, Mr. Rosen? I don't understand."

"That's why I was anxious to get hold of Sean because of this script."

"Script?"

"Yes, the script about Dr. Dee. Here I've been sitting on the fabulous fucking script and an equally fabulous contract, but when I called this Luvenstein to iron out the details, the number is disconnected. It's like the guy never existed."

"Did you try Sollows?"

"Sure. I couldn't get to talk to Sollows personally, but his people told me they've never even heard of the script."

"What?"

"So I did a bit of digging and guess what I found?"

"I don't know, what?"

"The script I have here is written by Edward Kelly."

"Kelly?"

"Yeah, that was Talbot's real name! "

"Talbot?"

"Are you a fucking parrot?" Rosen was agitated. "Listen, when I got the script it was in a big manila envelope, and it was mailed from England. I've got it right here. The return address is Wistan

Manor, West Dropsorrow, Sussex. Does that mean anything to you?"

"That's this address," said Tom in a hollow voice.

"Where you are now? What the fuck is going on, Tom?"

"I wish I knew, Mr. Rosen."

Tom hung up in a daze, got up, descended the stairs and rang the bell on the table in the hallway.

After a few seconds, the pleasant woman from the dining room appeared. "May I help you?"

"Yes. Could I see Mr. Kelly, please?"

"Mr. Kelly?"

"Yes, the manager."

"I'm sorry, sir, the manager's name is Hathaway. We don't have any Mr. Kelly on staff."

Tom stared at her blankly, and then, collecting his wits, told the woman that Sean would no longer be needing his room and that if she would open the door he would move Sean's bags into his own room.

"Very good, sir. Will you be dining with us this evening?"

"Yes, I guess so."

"Will the young lady be dining with you again, sir?"

"No. The young lady has gone."

50

Tom had almost no money left and could not afford to put more on his credit card. He had not been earning for the past several weeks and knew he had missed out on a number of productions for which he would have auditioned had he been at home. Moreover, the collapse of the Sollows movie—if it had ever existed in any form—had left him with no immediate prospects.

So he hitchhiked to Heathrow, and with great difficulty negotiated on foot the labyrinth of roads to the terminal. He caught his plane only in the nick of time.

When he reached Halifax some six hours later, he did not even have the price of a taxi, so waited for the airport bus. When finally he let himself into the apartment, he was broke, tired, angry and sick at heart.

After a few days of resting and a few more of looking for work, he resolved to track down Tamsin. He could not see her name on the website which listed Halifax telephone numbers, so he called the local ACTRA office, only to be told that the union had no record of such a person.

That night he went to the Economy Shoe Shop, but there was no sign of her. He asked around the tables, but nobody knew anything about her and had not seen anyone fitting her description. He returned on several other nights with similar results. Then he visited other bars in the city, asking bartenders if they had seen her. Nobody had noticed a ravishing young woman with bright red hair.

After some months had passed, Tom began to wonder if it had all been a dream. But the sensation of her wonderful body next to his and the sight of that exciting, flaming hair would not leave him. It never did.

51

After eight days had passed, Mr. Hartley-Simpson instructed that Sean be transferred to Meadowfield in Worthing. There was nothing more he could do for the patient, who acted as if he had dementia and no longer maintained any connection with the real world. He came to the conclusion that this was a serious and irreversible case.

At Meadowfield, Sean sat in bed all day looking straight ahead, not acknowledging anything which was done for him or said to him. His eyes were open most of the time, but he showed no indication of knowing or caring anything of his surroundings. Clearly, his mind was in some other place, a place where the wind...

LII

...blew cool and clean from the sea across the rolling downs as the last rays of the sun slipped from the darkening sky. A lonely, black-robed figure moved, with some inner purpose, over the crests of the downs, past the ancient stone circle, and away beyond it until it was merely a speck in the landscape.

Then it blended into the nothingness of the gathering night.

About the author

Jeremy Akerman is an adoptive Nova Scotian who has lived in the province since 1964. In that time he has been an archaeologist, a radio announcer, a politician, a senior civil servant, a newspaper editor and a film actor.

He is painter of landscapes and portraits, a singer of Irish folk songs, a lover of wine, and a devotee of history, especially of the British Labour Party.